THE HAUNTED
SOUL

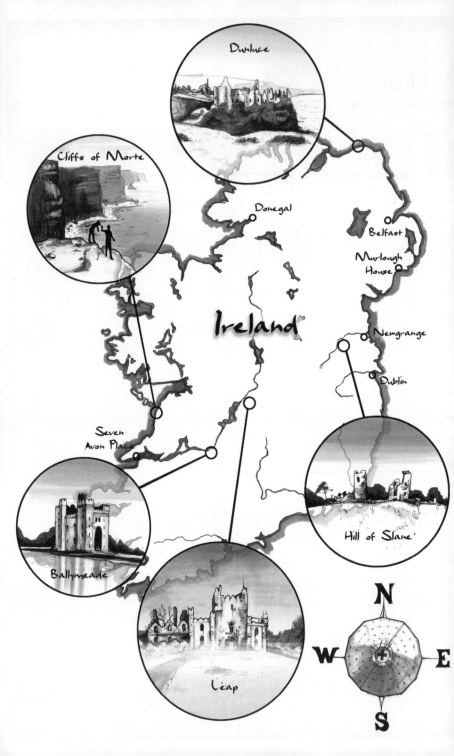

Dunluce

Cliffs of Morte

Donegal

Belfast

Murlough House

Ireland

Newgrange

Dublin

Seven Avon Place

Hill of Slane

Ballymeade

Leap

N

W   E

S

Elijah Creek & The Armor of God #5

THE HAUNTED SOUL

Lena Wood

✻✻✻✻✻✻✻✻✻✻

Standard
PUBLISHING
Bringing The Word to Life

Text © 2005 Lena Wood.
© 2005 Standard Publishing, Cincinnati, Ohio. A division of Standex
International Corporation. All rights reserved. Printed in USA.
Project editor: Lindsay Black
Content editor: Amy Beveridge
Copy editor: Lynn Lusby Pratt
Cover and interior design: Rob Glover
Cover oil paintings: Lena Wood
Map illustration: Daniel Armstrong

Library of Congress Cataloging-in-Publication Data

Wood, Lena, 1950-
  The haunted soul / Lena Wood.
    p. cm. — (Elijah Creek & the armor of God ; bk. 5)
  Summary: While traveling with his friends to Ireland in hopes of finding the
sword of truth, Elijah experiences haunting visions of lost souls and begins to
question his newfound faith in God.
  ISBN 0-7847-1760-5 (soft cover)
  [1. Christian life--Fiction. 2. Friendship--Fiction. 3. Ireland--Fiction.] I. Title.
PZ7.W84973Hau 2005
[Fic]--dc22

                                                              2005012797

                        ISBN 0-7847-1760-5

  02 01 00 09 08 07 06   9 8 7 6 5 4 3 2 1

to Lenora *and* Hudson,
the next wave

Deepest appreciation to:
Angie, Julie, Cynthia, Jacque, John,
and all the other kind folks
in Ireland
for steering me in the right direction

Family
for continuing support

&

El-Telan-Yah

You believe that there is one God. Good!
Even the demons believe that—and shudder.

—James 2:19

IT'S hard to say when I started to really believe in God. I guess I knew from when I was four years old down in Georgia and woke up in the middle of the night for no reason. I went out to the porch just in time to see lightning strike a tree. I kind of knew I was supposed to see it, so it didn't scare me. I didn't run inside and wake Mom—I never told anyone. Maybe it was him saying to me even way back then: *Know who you're dealing with, Elijah Creek.*

The armor quest and Reece's confidence in God pumped up my belief in him. Skid's Quella helped too. But what nailed it for me was what Dr. Eloise calls the Presence, the feeling I'd get that he was watching me from trees and sky—from everywhere; or when he stood by my side as real as Skid. I can't describe it except to say that it empties you out and fills you up at the same time. So I sort of always believed—kind of hard not to, really. Just look around.

God had to be the scariest being imaginable, scarier than all the terrors in the world combined. He was the Master of Breath with the power of the distant stars in his control.

So why would I want to be around him? That was the thing I couldn't get. I knew how dangerous he was—I'd seen it firsthand—but I was anxious to know him better, to move in closer. Why? Beats me, but there it is.

As for when I first believed in Satan, I can nail it down precisely: I was over three thousand miles from home on Halloween week of my freshman year. It was around 12:30.

Chapter 1

I was reaching my hand into the fire, trying to snatch something out of it. My mom screamed at me, but I kept saying, "I'm okay, I'm okay!" I wasn't being burned, but they didn't believe me. "I'm okay!" I insisted.

"Elijah?" Mom's worried voice called to me as if from far away. She shook me awake. "You were having a nightmare. Elijah, hon, it's all right. You're in your room."

I sat up—my head wobbling, my eyelids drooping.

"Dad needs you at the nature center right away, but it's not an emergency." She tousled my hair. "It's a *good* thing."

"'Kay." I forced my eyes open and surveyed the backyard. Through my open window, I saw the pool, as quiet and blue as the sky above. Beyond lay a plot of bare land. The Camp Mudjokivi trustees had bought up the spot that once was Old Pilgrim Church. Dad wanted to make it into a sand volleyball court—his idea being to attract college kids for twilight pool shindigs while campers trekked through Owl Woods on night hikes. I rubbed sleep from my eyes, threw back the covers, and stood, swaying like a drunk. "I'm okay."

Mom laughed. "You said that already. Dorian just called and asked me to drop by right away. He sounded mysterious on the phone." She walked out of the room, twisting her hair up and clipping it. "It's probably nothing. He loved teasing me as a kid. My brother, the bane of my existence!"

School was set to start in a week, and I dreaded it more than usual. The five of us had spent half the summer roaming Council Cliffs State Park. Roaming: it's what I like best in the world. Then Reece got hurt. The doctors had to cut a bone out of her leg, sand it off, and put it back in. Mei had been sent back to Japan by her parents, who thought we were some weird religious cult for kids. According to Reece, Mei's parents had found some ideas for clan names that Mei had written in her journal—names like Warriors of *Gi,* Fighters for God. To an outsider this might seem weird, but we were just regular kids looking for an old suit of armor with the power and history of spiritual warfare tied up in it. Mei's parents didn't understand. They tried to get her to break off from our group. When she wouldn't budge, they shipped her back to Japan.

Reece missed Mei a bunch, and our clan was down to four again: Reece, Skid, Rob, and me. I didn't get why God didn't fix everything. Several times I'd even asked, *Why are you doing this to Reece—taking her friends away, keeping her on crutches? She trusts you. You're number one with her. Doesn't that count for something?* I even said once, *Hey, if that's what it means to be on your A-Team, no thanks.*

Dad met me in the reptile room of the nature center, wearing his usual khakis and Camp Mudj T-shirt. "We have buyers, Elijah. The money's yours, son."

I perked up. "For the baby snakes? Cool!" We high fived. "Really?! How much?" I peeked in on the writhing mass of speckled blue racer babies, which were under maximum security alert with a padlocked cage and a sign on the reptile room door: "Authorized Personnel Only"—meaning Dad, Bo, and me.

Dad admired our stash of rare snakes. "We're still dickering on the price," he answered.

"Dicker high, okay?"

"You earned it, Elijah." He broke into a chuckle. "You know what *I'd* pay cold cash for: seeing you tear up the hill again—your fists full of baby blues—and Rob bounding sideways into the lake like a human pogo stick."

I thanked Dad again and headed back to the house. My dad's the greatest—ever. I want to make that clear before I tell this next part. I don't mean anything bad by this, but after that night earlier in the summer when he couldn't answer my questions about God and the other world out there, there was a shift in my thinking. Dad didn't have all the answers, especially answers to questions that I'd come to think were pretty important. I needed to know.

"Can I borrow that Quella sometime?" I asked Skid when we met by accident at the store. We were loading up on school supplies. The twins needed glue and colored pencils, and they'd graduated from round scissors to the pointy, dangerous ones. I hoped Mom was ready to part with her good drapes and anything else they could get a blade through.

"The Quella?" Skid asked. "Sure. Why?"

"Well," I stammered, getting shy all of a sudden, "you guys keep bugging me about church. I want to know what I'm getting into beforehand."

He pulled it out of his jacket pocket and handed it over. "Look up *saved,* Creek. That's what you're shooting for."

"Okay. Thanks."

Later that week—almost a year since we'd first gone into Old Pilgrim Church—I went up on Devil's Cranium and built a little fire, just enough to read by. This wasn't a vision quest; I was learning that God's showing up didn't depend on you sweating and showering and starving yourself. You could knock yourself out, and he might leave you sitting there in the dead quiet to think it out all alone. It was his call. Reece thought he'd be showing up in the Word to tell us what to do next, which was good enough for me.

It was funny, reading about saved in the Bible. There were a bunch of short paragraphs in different parts to hunt down and ponder a long time. It wasn't like a schoolbook. Learning about saved was kind of like my first prayer walk, only I wasn't walking a snake-infested meadow at dawn.

"He will save his people from their sins," I read.

Sins? Well, God, I used to lie, but I've steered away from it after finding the belt of truth. As for other sins, I haven't killed anyone except Salem. I haven't stolen anything except for that leather key ring from Mitts Bros. Department Store when Aunt Grace worked there. Once was all, and I lost the key ring the next day at school. I was seven and dumb at the time. Sorry 'bout that.

"Whoever wants to save his life will lose it, but whoever loses his life for me will find it."

Huh? What's that mean? I'll have to ask Reece or Skid.

I read, "What good is it, my brothers, if a man claims to have faith but has no deeds? Can such faith save him?" and "For it is by grace you have been saved, through faith."

Then in the book of Romans, it said, "If you confess with your mouth, 'Jesus is Lord,' and believe in your heart that God raised him from the dead, you will be saved." I considered the words in the mellow twilight of late summer.

From high on Devil's Cranium, I looked across Telanoo, which I had fully claimed as my own. No one else wanted it, no one used it, and I'd covered pretty much all of it looking for the armor. If I got creeped out—like the time I heard a coyote at sundown on the west perimeter, or the time of the deep fog when I lost my way—I'd call to El-Telan-Yah: a name I made meaning "the God of Telanoo is Yahweh."

School started. Our moms got it into their heads from the PTO meetings that we each needed to build "a well-rounded academic and extracurricular portfolio in order to have an impressive college application." Translation: get involved in clubs and sports. After my experience with last year's crop of college-age camp counselors (slimeball creatures of the night, according to Rob), I wasn't spotting any ivy-covered halls of higher learning on my horizon. The only things the counselors had taught me was how to catch poison ivy, how to build illegal fires in a state park, and how never to get asked to work at Camp Mudj again. No thanks.

But our moms wouldn't budge, so Rob signed on to the swim team, school newspaper staff, and drama club. Skid went out for tennis and Spanish club. Reece got into choir and started her own girls' Christian club called Devo. I joined the cross-country team. It was no surprise as school got underway that powwow time was going to be harder to come by.

I even broke down and took a language class. Magdeline Independent didn't offer Hebrew or Greek, which I was now interested in because of the armor and the Quella. The closest option was Latin, which Mom said would help me speak English better. That made no sense, but I didn't want to argue with Mom over a dumb thing like school. So I signed on.

We freshmen were given a red alert about the Latin teacher, Miss Abner, but upperclassmen tended to use scare tactics to keep the upper hand. Supposedly her classes were sheer terror. I couldn't picture it. She was ancient, less than five feet tall, and blind as a bat. She wore pink and purple every day and wore her hair combed up and piled on her head like a plate of gray sausages. People said that she wore contact lenses with her glasses but still couldn't see. And if she heard talking during class, she'd just send a random person to the office. You could be the next victim! Seniors claimed that she knew Latin because she had dated Caesar.

Miss Abner admitted all of her shortcomings on the first day of class. She sat behind her big desk, rubbing her hands together like a fly does before it starts in on a dead squirrel. "My faculties aren't what they used to be," she said in an uppity, high-pitched voice. "I can't see well, my hearing has deteriorated, and they tell me my reflexes have slipped," she smiled out the window, "but at least I can still drive."

We laughed uncertainly. Was that supposed to be a joke?

Her head bobbed at each of us as if she were counting us. She made a thin, straight smile. "However, my teaching skills have not depreciated in the least since I entered the teaching profession right after the war."

Someone behind me whispered, "Trojan War."

"Your test over chapter one is on the board. Begin."

We first-day Latin students—there were only thirteen of us—traded terrified glances. *Hey, did I miss something here? A test? This is the first day, isn't it?!*

Dora Ann, a straight-A student who regularly cheated to keep her grades up, raised a trembling hand. "Miss Abner, this is our first class. I just got my textbook this morning!"

Miss Abner bent her rigid neck at Dora Ann. "Didn't all of you just come from study hall?" she surveyed us knowingly. "I expect my students to come prepared *every* day!"

Basketball player Mike—big, blond, red-cheeked,

and meek as a lamb—raised his hand. "Well, ma'am, we just didn't know that. Our other teachers usually give us *assignments* on the first day and tests *after* we've studied those assignments."

Obviously Miss Abner didn't like being compared to the other teachers. And she didn't like Mike insinuating that she didn't know the teaching business. She pushed back her chair, stood, and whirled to the board. She grabbed up a piece of chalk and drew angry circles around the test questions. Then she turned and squinted at us. Surrounded by a white halo of chalk and with meanness written all over her face, Miss Abner bobbed her head at us maliciously. "You shall not do well in my class if you are not prepared!"

In the cafeteria Rob's table was full of guys, so I slid my lunch tray across from Reece and said hey. She was in the process of sitting down by Emma Stone, a tall freshman with choppy, brown hair and cute freckles across her nose. I said, "Hi, Emma. Same lunch time. Cool." Since Mei was gone, Reece had chummed up with Emma. She was bubbly and friendly enough, but nosy and a big talker—not at all like Mei. I could tell that she was just a stand-in best friend.

Reece slid her crutches under the table. "I'd ask you to get my tray, Elijah, but the guys would call you a wimp or worse."

"I'll get it," Emma said and took off.

Reece called after her, "Pizza, salad, two milks, no cake."

The three of us talked over lunch about the usual stuff—

what classes we liked and which teachers spelled trouble with a capital *T.* "Abner," I said dejectedly. "She's everything they say and more. We had a test already. I flunked. She even spied out our schedules and knows when we have study hall!"

Reece was shocked. "Are you serious?" She huffed sympathetically at me and then narrowed her eyes at Miss Abner, who was hunched over in the teachers' corner. "Peanut butter and crackers—that's all she eats. They say that she drives on the wrong side of the road because she can't see."

A guy down the table jumped in. "She drives the biggest Caddy ever made, and last year it came at me on Scioto Road—a big, white barge and nobody behind the wheel!"

"What do you mean?" Reece asked.

"Oh, she was driving, all right. But Abner's so short that she has to look through the steering wheel!" He shuddered. "I hit the ditch, cracked my windshield, and knocked my wheels out of line. And she kept right on driving!" He tossed his fork down angrily. "The cops won't stop her. *They* all had her for Latin when *they* were in high school! She's untouchable!"

"No kidding," I said seriously.

When Emma left for class and the table thinned out, I saw my chance. "Hey, Reece, um, I borrowed Skid's Quella and read some of it last night."

She perked up. "Really?"

"I read up on saved."

"Want to take the plunge?"

When I paused, she smiled at me, "Elijah, it's only a matter of time. It'd be nice if you had faith before we found the shield of faith. You'd be ahead for once."

"If I wanted to, how would I do it?"

"What'd the Quella say to do?"

"A bunch of stuff."

"Like what?"

I shrugged. "Believe."

"Done. You do believe in God, right?"

"Kind of hard not to, since—" I lowered my voice, "we're looking for his armor."

"What else?"

"It says to confess with your mouth and call on God's name, be baptized, stand firm to the end, repent, something about grace. One part was about losing my life to find it— that doesn't mean dying, does it?"

Reece popped the last bite of pizza into her mouth and shook her head. "Living sacrifice. It means following God no matter what." She thought for a second. "But it *could* mean dying. Some of Jesus' followers were killed because they believed."

"Like the Moravian Delawares," I remembered.

"Yes, and for thousands of years before them. Millions have died because of their faith in God. The Stallards told us that." She blotted her mouth, wadded the napkin, and tossed it onto her plate. Then she clasped her hands under her chin and gave me a huge smile. "I really admire you for being the first one in your family. You're a man of courage, Elijah."

Reece Elliston was the prettiest girl I'd ever seen, and I was so busy looking at her that I hardly caught what she said next: "I can tell you right now that you won't be living the regular life: go to church on Sunday, put a buck in the offering plate, and light a candle at Christmas. Nope."

"Uh-huh."

"The real journey is scary."

"Yeah," I agreed, clueless.

"You need to meet with my minister right away."

"Minister? Okay. But first I should talk to my parents."

"And church is cool once you get used to it."

"This week? There's no rush, is there?" I asked uneasily.

Reece huffed at me. "There may be." All of a sudden she was squishy again. Her eyes went melty. She squeezed my hand, snuck her hand back in her lap, and glanced around shyly. "I'm so proud of you."

I don't know why it was so hard to bring up the subject of my beliefs. Dad was busy, and I didn't think Mom would understand. So I waited and followed Dad down to the lake that night. We talked about nothing until it got quiet. He gave me a quizzical look. "What is it, Elijah?"

"It's something I've been thinking about for a while. About giving my life to God."

Dad nodded. It was his cautious nod. "I see. I know many good people who are religious. Reece is, isn't she?"

"That's not the reason."

"All right. May I ask why you're thinking about this?"

"Lots of reasons, I guess." I looked out over the lake to Owl Woods. "He made the world—Camp Mudj and the wind and waves and trees and everything. He tells nature what to do, and it does it. I've seen it happen, Dad. And I've been out there at night with no one around, and he's there. I can't explain it. He—" I didn't know how far to go with this. I wanted to tell Dad about how he talks to me and the others through the Quella and the silence and sometimes in a strong, quiet voice. But I didn't want Dad thinking of me the same way Mei's parents did. "He just wants me to, that's all."

"And how will you go about it?"

"Reece is going to have her minister talk to me. I'll have to start going to her church, but they'll give me a ride."

"I don't see any harm in going to church. But we'll discuss it with your mom first."

Mom wasn't totally keen on my being a Christian, but said I was getting old enough to make my own decisions. She made it clear I was still "accountable" to them and that church shouldn't take up all my time or interfere with my schoolwork. She also asked why. It was hard to say what I'd been through the past year. My parents thought the Stallards were weird. They were right, but weird didn't always mean bad. Weird could be cool if God had something to do with it.

That very next night, Reece's mom drove us to her church. Their minister was the guy who'd had the great sermon about Indians, so I wasn't nervous to talk to him. We sat in his office in a circle of big fake-leather chairs, just him and me and Reece who was beaming from ear to ear. He showed me some of the same verses I'd found in the Quella.

"I've read those," I said.

"Good! You've already done your homework about becoming a Christian."

I gulped. "There's homework!?"

Reece cracked up.

"Oh, there's homework, all right," he chuckled, "but God gives the tests. And they're usually pop quizzes."

Visions of Abner flickered before me, and I shuddered.

"From what Reece told me, Elijah, you've already passed a few of those tests. You're the first in your family?"

"Yessir."

"We need to make this official, and then you can keep on with what you've started. First and foremost, this isn't about following a man's list of rules to live by. It's committing to a relationship with the living God."

"Okay," I agreed.

He looked at me thoughtfully. "Have you been attending a church regularly?"

"No. Just the time you preached about the Indians and once in a pentecoastal church in South Carolina."

"Pentecoastal?"

I shrugged. "That's what they called it. There was a lot of yelling and crying and dancing, but it was okay."

He smiled at Reece. "He's open-minded. I like that. So, Elijah, what made you decide to become a Christian?"

"Reece and Skid and . . . God himself. He called me."

He looked a little stunned. "Wow." He sat back in his chair and gave me a look so curious it was scary. "He called you."

"Yessir."

"How'd that happen?"

I didn't want to tell how God told me to find the armor and how I'd figured that God needed me to be on his side. "It's kind of personal," I answered, glancing at Reece, "but it's true. He called me."

"Wow," he said again. "Perhaps we'll talk about that in the future."

I said okay, but hoped he'd be too busy or forget about it. It would be almost impossible to tell my story without spilling the beans about the armor.

He called my parents to be sure it was okay for me to make this decision. Then he explained the drill for Sunday morning: I'd have to come up in front of everyone, but only to answer a few questions and prove I was serious. Then I'd be baptized, dunked under water as a sign that I was dead to my old life and starting a new one. (When Reece had mentioned my taking the plunge, I didn't know she meant literally.)

The minister prayed for me, and Reece got all teary-eyed.

Skid knew the drill about getting dunked. Rob bugged me for details with a shifty look in his eyes, and I wondered if he was thinking about becoming an official believer too.

That Sunday I dressed up in my one white shirt and the new pants Mom bought for the occasion. Then I was really nervous. Skid's family was there even though this wasn't their regular church. Rob sat by himself in the back and sneaked out a couple of times to get a drink and go to the restroom. It made me feel good, his being nervous on my big day.

Reece and her mom were there with Officer Taylor. Seeing him and Reece's mom give each other goo-goo eyes was traveling-freak-show weird, so I didn't watch.

The sermon started, and Reece whispered, "When they sing the last song, you go. I'll come with you if you want."

"I can handle it," I said, acting brave.

Leading herds of kids on night hikes or wrestling a handful of baby snakes seemed like no big deal compared to walking up in front of hundreds of strangers. It gave me the willies, but it was too late to back out.

When the sermon ended and the time came, the music sounded way far off like I was in a bubble. The first verse was over, and they went into the chorus. Reece nudged me and smiled, "It's now or never."

Stepping out, I went a little bit blank. But in no time I was standing at the front, looking at a sea of faces. The minister put his arm around my shoulder and introduced me as a friend of the Elliston family. Mom and Dad watched me from the back with a kind of sad pride as if they were thinking, *It could be worse; he could be out stealing hubcaps.*

I said aloud that I believed Jesus was the Son of God and that I wanted him to save me from my sins and be the Lord of my life. Then I was taken to a back room where I stripped down to my underwear and put on a white robe while organ music droned in the auditorium. Then someone started singing a song that was perfect for me, about running a race and asking the Spirit to fall like fire and rain. A guy knocked on the door of the dressing room, and I went out. In front of everyone, I stepped down into a big tank of warm water where the minister was waiting for me with waders on. He turned me around, and that's when I caught a glimpse of something yellow floating on the water.

The minister said, "Elijah Creek, do you believe that Jesus is the Christ, the Son of the living God?"

A yellow rubber ducky bobbed toward me from the edge of the baptistery. Peeking around the corner from the backstage part of the baptistery was a fuzzy, blond head and one big, prankish eye.

You're dead, Wingate. Dead!

I had rehearsed what I was supposed to say, but my train of thought derailed. "Umm . . ." A hundred ideas flipped through my mind. If the audience saw me with a rubber ducky on my holy dunking, I'd never live it down. I'd have to convert to another religion. My best idea was to go under fast and hard enough to make a tidal wave and send the thing back to its corner. "Amen!" I threw myself backward with a splash. Before I went under, the minister blurted, "I now bap—!"

I forgot to close my mouth. It was over in a second, and I came up sputtering, dripping wet. But my tidal wave had worked; the ducky listed toward the corner of the baptistery.

The minister frowned at me and stammered, "I now . . . I just . . . I have baptized you in the name of the Father and the Son and the Holy Spirit. Amen."

I'd jumped the gun on his ceremony and went under too soon. *Did it take?* Snickers came from the top of the steps. *Not funny, Rob Wingate! You just wait . . . uh-oh . . .* The ducky had bumped the wall and was heading back. I slapped at the water, hoping to change its course. The minister thought I was panicking again. He patted my back reassuringly and whispered, "It's okay, son. You're okay."

I wiped water from my face. *Oh brother! Those people out there think I clammed up, that I'm afraid of three feet of water! Dad'll never let me lifeguard at Camp Mudj, ever again! Wingate, you are so dead!*

Strange, that my first thought as an official sin-free Christian was to murder my cousin in cold blood.

People clapped like I'd done something great. The minister said I'd now have a new life. I didn't hear angels sing or anything. I didn't feel much different other than being wet and ticked off at Rob. But I'd taken the plunge, and things would be different now, I guessed. Once I got changed and the last prayer was said, I stood down front with my parents and the minister. Everyone came by and shook my hand. Some people I'd never met hugged me and said welcome. It was kind of like when Grandma plants a wet kiss on your cheek: icky but nice.

Reece crowded in line and hugged me hard. She whispered, "It's okay that you got choked up. I cried too!" She hugged me again right in front of everyone.

Chapter 2

ON Monday, my life was full steam ahead for God (except for a dark plot stewing in the back of my mind on how to get even with Rob). But scheduling powwows suddenly had a new complication: Emma Stone. She hung around all the time and wasn't like Mei, who would give somebody a minute of privacy with Reece. I knew without asking that it was only a matter of time before Reece would want to bring her into the circle.

When Emma went to get Reece's lunch tray, I mentioned, "Hey, you're not telling her anything about . . . you know."

"No," Reece said glumly. "But I wish I had someone to talk to about it."

"You have us guys," I defended.

She shook her head. "It's not the same."

"We need a powwow. How about Tuesday? We could have it at your house . . . if the lovebirds aren't there," I said, teasing her about her mom and Officer Taylor. We compared schedules. Reece said, "Tuesday would work."

"Work for what?" Emma sat Reece's tray down.

Instantly I had a made-up answer: Mom needed Reece to baby-sit. But I couldn't lie. "Some of us hang out every now and then," I said casually.

"I'm free on Tuesday," Emma said.

While Emma dug into her lunch, Reece and I argued with our eyes: hers were asking, *Is there a possibility we could bring her in?* My eyes answered, *Not a chance.*

Somehow during the year, with all the publicity and the police storming Camp Mudj over church burnings, mysterious fires, grave diggings, and journals stolen from the police department—not to mention the Kate Dowland mystery and the very belt of truth in custody for a while—somehow we'd kept the armor of God a secret from the world. And that's how it would have to be. My eyes told Reece, *We can't risk it.*

Hers said in a lonely way, *I know.*

I said to Emma, "Rob may have a club on Tuesday. (This was true.) I'll have to get back to you."

That very day Reece, Rob, and I found notes on our lockers in Skid's handwriting: *POWWOWASAP.*

We settled on the Tree House Village at 9:00 that night. All the tree houses were under roof but hadn't passed city inspection yet; we wouldn't be bothered.

The three of us had just gathered when Skid swooped in on his skateboard. Halfway down the path to the lake, he pulled a piece of paper out of his pocket and waved it in the air. At breakneck speed he zipped around the lake, ditched the board, and flew up the steps to the tree house. "I have a letter, people, and wait until you hear! We be gettin' some praise on!" He dropped down cross-legged and read:

*Dear Children, We pray you are doing well in your first year of
high school. Here's what we have on the shoes. It's obvious they are
not from the Roman era but of Spanish origin. As to how they were
engraved with* Langundowagan, *the Delaware Indian word for
"peace," here are our theories:*

*In the early days of America, native peoples were sometimes
taken to Europe, either by force as a curiosity to the conquerors, or
voluntarily to get an education. Perhaps a Native American picked
up these sandals in Europe in the eighteenth century where he heard
the gospel. Upon his return to America—or at his death—he left
his sandals behind in Europe, engraved with his native word for
"peace" as a witness to his faith. Another spiritual warrior wore the
sandals to Ireland where they joined the rest of the armor.*

*A more likely possibility is that these shoes belonged to Cabeza
de Vaca, whom we mentioned before. In 1528 his boat ran aground
near what is now Galveston, Texas. He met gentle tribes and
preached the gospel of peace when many churchmen were adding
to their numbers by cruel force. De Vaca went back to Spain, then
South America, then back to Europe where he died. Since the
Renaissance was a time of global travel, it's not a far stretch that
the next owner of the shoes went to the British Isles, i.e., Ireland,
where Dowland eventually purchased the full armor. This is the
strongest Native American connection we have found.*

*Children, we realize that the shoes are perhaps the least
glamorous of all the armor pieces, but certain hunters of religious
or Indian relics might want them for the historical significance.
Yes, we do keep saying that the armor is not worth a great deal as*

a relic, but the world of archaeology is an unpredictable market. Items which had been gathering dust on our shelves for decades have recently caught the eye of certain collectors. All the more reason to keep the search to ourselves.

Skid looked up, said, "Okay, here's where it starts getting good," and continued:

On another matter . . . all of you—but especially Elijah— seemed upset about the missing sword. What we feared about the sword may be true. From what we can deduce, there was a sword during the time of Paul. We may even trace a sketchy trail all the way back to creation. After sin entered the world, the Garden of Eden was barred from humankind with a fiery, ever-turning instrument of war. It must have been a perilous-looking thing, double-edged and glittering, a brandishing, slashing, thrusting weapon, even more terrifying in that it accompanied the mystical angel-beasts known as cherubim. The sword, which represented God's word of judgment, was apparently visible at that time. Whether it was a physical sword can't be determined. (Occasionally—and not always pleasantly—the senses are exposed to this parallel universe we called the spiritual realm.)

Why it is not with the rest of the armor is most vexing. On a positive note: a "sword of flame" is described in a few little-known writings from around the world, and depicted in certain carvings and tapestries from abroad. Whether their inspiration was the actual sword itself is currently our most perplexing question.

Skid looked up. "Okay, now it gets to us."

We have a hint of a sword around 400 AD in Ireland and

wending its way across Europe through the Middle Ages and then back again. The sword seemed to appear in concurrence with the renewed interest in the Word of God.

Here is our plan. Skid paused and grinned. *We must start in Ireland right away. We have written to your parents in a separate mailing to ask permission and will do the same for your school. We are calling it an educational and cultural tour, which it most certainly is. Any of your parents is welcome to chaperone since they do not all entirely trust us. Please move quickly on passports. Rest assured that we will keep costs at a minimum. In the meantime would you look through the journals or contact Francine Dowland to get the name of the castle where the armor was purchased? We must know where we're going in order to get there!*

All Our Best,
The Stallards

Skid raised the letter and let it drift down on the breeze. Then he sat back, proud as a peacock—like he had something to do with it.

I couldn't believe my ears. "Ireland? They mean it?"

Skid punched his fists into the night sky. "To the Emerald Isle, my people!"

Eyes bugged, Rob said, "They already asked our parents?!"

I glanced at Reece. A look of doubt clouded her face. "Wait!" she said. "Shouldn't we check Dowland's house first? I mean, we never did, and the sword could be hidden in a dark corner. Actually the next piece is the shield of faith and then the helmet. The sword is last. I'll bet Darrell—I mean Officer Taylor—could get us into Dowland's house."

Rob said, "Remember what Francine said? There was no sword with Dowland's armor."

Skid huffed, "The Stallards don't give up so easily."

Reece was the least pumped about going to Ireland to search for the sword of the Lord. I wondered if her mom had the money. I worried that Reece didn't have the strength.

We made our way back around the lake, chattering about whether we'd get in trouble with God if we found the pieces out of order and about going back to the old Dowland place. The first chance I got, I pulled Reece aside and whispered, "About Ireland—it's like that time at Devil's Cranium when we all wanted to get to the ruin, but you didn't think you could make it. Remember what I said then: If I'm going, you're going."

She smiled weakly. "I hope so."

I called Francine several times, but no one answered. I wondered if she was on vacation, or sick. Or dead. After a few days, I ran by the police station to ask Officer Taylor if he knew anything. In the meantime Reece went through the Dowland journals for a clue about where to start once we got to Ireland. When she turned up nothing, Rob went over them again. He'd already been studying maps of Ireland, getting familiar with place names. "If a place is referenced in the journals, I'll spot it," he said with confidence.

By pure miracle our parents gave the go-ahead. Aunt Grace was to chaperone and do research for her tea room. We were to leave the last week in October if all our paperwork came in.

We had a ton of things to talk about every day, but Emma ate with Reece and kept prying about when we could all hang out. Don't get me wrong; she was nice and cute too. But when it came out that the four of us were going to Ireland, she'd be on us like scum on a pond. Her parents were both doctors; she'd be able to scrounge up money for a plane ticket. As for me, I used the snake money to help pay for mine—funny how things work out sometimes.

Reece hadn't given us guys her final word on Ireland, and my attempts to keep Emma out of the loop were wearing thinner by the day. I strong-armed Rob into giving up lunch at the guys' table to start eating with us. I needed help in the chitchat department to keep Reece in top-secret mode.

We talked grades. "I have two big fat Fs in Latin already! All I've learned so far is Caesar's motto. It looks like this—" I wrote on a napkin *Veni, Vidi, Vici,* "which means, 'I came, I saw, I conquered.' But in old Latin when all the *V*s were *W*s, it comes out weeny, weedy, weeky."

Reece cackled. "What kind of a wimpy motto is that?!"

Rob said, "Sounds Hawaiian," and proceeded to stand up and go into a hula dance, singing, "Weeky weeky weeny weedy wooky cooky hooky," and so on until the whole cafeteria thought he was freshman psycho of the year.

Skid saw the proceedings and sauntered over to our table. Reece was dying laughing as she said, "You're embarrassing us, Rob. Why don't you go back to the guys' table?"

Skid leaned coolly over to Rob. "You danced a beansy weansy hula for the masses at Magdeline High. You can never go back."

I thought Aunt Grace was going to Ireland with us until one night after dinner. My bedroom window was open, and I heard Mom ask Dad if she could go to Ireland instead of Aunt Grace. I stuck my head out. "That'd be cool!"

She viped up at me. "Elijah, you weren't supposed to be listening!" She poked Dad playfully in the chest. "Your son has radar." Then she turned to me, "Not a word, you hear?"

October rolled on with no news on Francine, which had me worried. Reece was still on crutches and tight-lipped about going to Ireland. My cross-country coach was miffed about my leaving the country. "You got talent, Creek," he'd said when I broke the news. "But you can't come in here, show your stuff, and . . ." He'd shoved his hands roughly into his pockets. "I may have to rethink you. Lack of commitment is bad for morale."

I had to be doing something about the next piece of armor. On a blustery October Saturday, I gathered our clan of four at Dowland's place, 26 Jewett Avenue in Newpoint. Officer Taylor had cleared it for us to have a last look around the house before it went up for auction. Two men were there, appraising the contents of the house.

"Shield *and* helmet *and* right arm," Rob whispered as we split up for the search, each one to a room.

"And sword," I reminded.

"Francine said there was no sword," said Rob flatly. "It's still in Ireland."

"We don't know that. She and Stan split up years ago, remember? He may have gone back to Ireland to find it!"

Deep down I wanted the sword to be in Ireland so we could go on an awesome trip and find it there. But I didn't want Reece fretting herself into a relapse over it. "We'll look around here. Clean sweep—don't miss a spot."

I took the dining room, a small room with a pine table, a hutch painted blue, and an old mahogany desk with one drawer. The hutch had the usual: dishes on the top shelves, tablecloths and stuff stored in the bottom cabinet. I nosed around and checked for secret compartments.

Reece came into the room. "Nothing in the kitchen but cookware. The pantry's almost bare. Can I help you look?"

"Nothing here. Did you check for secret compartments?"

"No, but I didn't see anything unusual."

I saw my chance. "Reece . . . about Ireland . . . your mom's going to let you go, isn't she?" It was my way of putting it nice, but cut-to-the-chase Elliston didn't let me get by.

"What you're asking is whether I'll be well enough."

"Yeah, that's what I mean. Are Skid and I going to be hauling you around a whole country on a stretcher?"

She smiled. "That's better. I'm in therapy, hoping I can get down to using a cane. Mom and I are praying every day. You pray too."

"Don't try so hard that you relapse." I fiddled through a drawer of maps and papers and other junk. "I . . . really want you to go." It was then that my hand hit something: a gun. I pulled it out and laid it on my palm. The words "Victor 22 Cal.R.F." were inscribed on the barrel.

Reece and I locked eyes. "A gun!" she cried.

In a flash I remembered how Stan Dowland had written my name three times in his journal and crossed it off twice. I couldn't help wondering whether he'd carried this weapon when he stalked me.

"A gun?" an appraiser came from the living room.

I offered it to him. "It was in a drawer behind the papers."

He looked it over. "Huh. Twenty-two caliber, cracked handle, probably works okay. Not worth much, but I'll have Norton take a look at it." He headed toward the bedroom calling, "Norton, we missed a gun." He turned to me and nodded approvingly. "Thanks."

The four of us gathered back in the living room empty-handed.

Rob said, "The boxes in his closet were just old taxes and clothes." He looked around the living room at the piles of magazines and papers. We could go through these."

Reece said, "That would take forever."

"We should shake out a few," he insisted, "to see if he hid clues or a map between the pages."

Skid said, "The bathroom and spare bedroom are no-shows. What about the basement?"

"Check it out, will you?" I answered. "Reece and I will go through some of these stacks."

"Aye, aye, Cap'n," Skid said. "Wingate, give me a hand."

Reece and I stayed busy, but we were both thinking the same thing. If she really couldn't go to Ireland, would I stay behind too, like I'd said? I'd thought hard about it and reasoned that if I was now a man of God, I had to be a man of my word. No matter how much it hurt. "About Ireland," I said quietly, "I meant what I said."

"That's what worries me," she said without looking up.

In a few minutes, Skid and Rob came pounding up the steps. Rob huffed, "Shelves of jars, a table full of dead plants under the back window, a couple of old mattresses."

I perked up. "Mattresses?"

Skid shook his head. "I thought the same thing, but we pressed on them and checked for rips or new stitching. Nothing stashed there. Nada."

"Anybody check the attic?" I asked.

Rob said, "The appraisers have been up there raking through the insulation. Lots of people hide treasures and documents in their attics, but it's empty."

"You're sure? They missed a gun, you know."

Rob slumped. "If you want to go up there and get itchy and have spiders drop on you or get bird lice and have to go get medication, go right ahead."

Skid's smiling, green eyes slid from Rob to me. "Voice of experience."

"The garage," I said. "Let's check there."

Reece stood slowly. "If we don't find anything, don't be discouraged. We're getting our directions from God now, not Dowland."

I unlocked the door to the garage, opened it, and sighed. "There's nothing here. The car's gone. The burlap sacks are gone. He already buried the pieces." We wandered out to the backyard, a small lot that slanted up to a fence surrounded by trees and thick shrubs. "Maybe he hid them in there."

Rob said, "If we're supposed to look for the shield of faith in the opposite place—a place of doubt—his home would be the spot, all right."

"We're not following Dowland anymore," Reece insisted.

"But he's the one who hid the armor," Rob argued.

I strolled to the edge of the property and hooked my fingers through the chain-link fence. "What other clues do we have?" I peered through the fence into the underbrush. No disturbed ground. No lingering smell of fresh dirt. "Nothing here," I said with confidence.

We stood in the tree-rimmed yard, empty-handed. "God's supposed to tell us," Reece kept saying.

"How?" I asked.

"Let's think. And pray," she said. "You go first."

"What?" I asked.

"Pray. You're a Christian now."

"You mean out loud?"

Skid smirked, "Or use smoke signals."

Reece herded us into a circle. I shoved my hands into my pockets and dropped my head. "Okay." I cleared my throat. "Okay, God. We're standing here in Dowland's backyard in Newpoint—"

Skid snickered. "He doesn't need latitude and longitude, Creek. He's God."

Reece hissed, "Shhh!" but I couldn't let it pass.

Head still bowed but eyes on Skid's lower half, I brought my foot up behind his knee and yanked, throwing him off balance. His head shot up. He grabbed my sleeve. I threw him off. He regained his balance and lunged for me. I took off for the fence. Rob burst out laughing.

Reece yelled, "You guys!! Cut it out! This is prayer time!"

Skid hollered, "He's gonna need prayer!"

Adrenaline rushed through me. I grabbed the fence with one hand; my feet scrambled up, got wings, and sailed over. I turned around victoriously. Skid slammed his palms into the fence, defeated but grinning. He was thinking up a wisecrack when Reece butted in. "Let's just go back to Council Cliffs."

I climbed back over the fence. "We've wandered around those hills long enough."

Chapter 2

"The raven is our only sign," she said in a frustrated tone. "God won't answer our prayers if we're not serious."

"I'm serious," I said. "Do you always have to stand still when you pray? Can't you pray on the move?" I thought a moment. "We've gone through those hills long enough."

"You just said that," she griped.

"I know," I said curiously, "but it seems important." The words echoed in my head again.

Reece asked, "What do you mean?"

"I don't know . . . hey . . . the trunk of his car! If he hasn't buried the pieces, they may be in the trunk."

Skid nodded. "Worth a shot."

I said, "Rob, go ask the appraisers where the car is."

While we waited for him, I caught Reece staring at me. She said, "Say it again."

"We've looked through those hills long enough?"

Reece turned to Skid. "Got the Quella? Look up 'hills' and 'long enough.'"

Skid said, "Okay. Here's what I have: 'Then the LORD said to me, "You have made your way around this hill country long enough; now turn north."'"

Rob came huffing and puffing across the yard. "They had it towed to a junkyard."

"Where?"

"North of here on Highway 137."

Chapter 3

CHILLS went down my spine. "North . . . how far?"

"About a mile."

I took off.

"Wait!" Reece said. "Skid's mom is on her way!"

"Tell her to pick me up at the junkyard!"

Reece called to me again, but I was already over the rise of Crayford Avenue. "Cross-country training!" I yelled back. A feeling of urgency and dread swept through me. "Now turn north," came the words of the Bible. *Now.*

Halfway there I noticed a pillar of blue smoke. The dream came back: me reaching into the fire, mom yelling, me shouting, "I'm okay!"

North. I sped, gulped air. Cars sped past. My feet pounded pavement. I wheeled into the junkyard and crashed through the door of an office not much bigger than a gatehouse. The man inside was looking through a grimy notebook. He jumped. "What the—!"

"You got a car here from Stan Dowland? From his estate? You would have just gotten it, an old blue sedan—"

"Yeah, yeah." He seemed annoyed that I'd scared him.

"I need something out of it. Did you know that there's a fire out there? Can't tell if it's on your property, but you may want to check it out."

Chapter 3

He came out of his run-down office cussing. "People burning off weeds in this wind. Idiots!"

"Where's the car?" I asked. "There may be something important in the trunk!"

He was paying attention to the smoke. "Grass fire." He muttered more curses. "Looks like it's come over my line. It'll smoke out the rats. We'll be crawling with 'em."

"The car!" I asked again.

He dialed the fire station, gave his location, slammed the phone, and took off down the dirt road. "Grab a shovel!"

By the time we'd reached the back of the junkyard, the smoke had grown to black billows stinking of burning rubber. The fire had reached a stack of tires. "You stay back," he ordered. He cussed at the rats scampering our way and batted them off the path with his shovel. "We got trouble."

"I have to look in Dowland's car," I insisted.

"Not if it's near the fire. I haven't siphoned the gas out."

Here came a handful of men alongside the burning field, waving shovels. Desperately I scanned the lot for Dowland's dusty-blue wreck.

"Where is it!?" I demanded. Then I saw it just beyond the burning tires. A siren wailed in the distance, but there wasn't time. Flames filled the windows of the car and licked the ground underneath. The tires smoldered and hissed. I ran toward it.

"Get back, kid! It could explode any minute!" he yelled.

I got as close as I could and looked inside. A window shattered from the heat. Flames bellowed out in my direction. I reeled backward. The seats were ablaze. The junkyard man drew his shovel in front of me. "Get back!"

"I have to check the trunk!" I ran to the back of the car, aimed the point of my shovel at the lock, and rammed.

"This could blow, you fool!" he screamed.

"I'm okay!" I yelled. I aimed and rammed again and then again. "I'm okay!" My hearing went into radar mode, each sound separate and distinct: the crackling of the flames, the hissing of tires, the boiling smoke, sirens and fire engine horns blaring, then a car horn and people screaming.

I rammed the shovel once more, and it stuck. I put my whole weight into it and pushed. *Crack!* The handle broke. In shock I stumbled backward. *No good!* The blade was still lodged under the trunk lid. I threw down the handle and looked around frantically for another tool.

"What are you doing, kid?!" came the voice of the junkyard man behind me. "Trying to kill yourself? Whatever's in there isn't worth it."

Leverage. I need leverage. I grabbed a cement block with one hand and yanked for all I was worth. *Got it!* I flew toward Dowland's car, winding up for a throw as I went. Somehow I swung that block in a perfect arc over my head. It came down with a blow dead on the shovel head with such force that the tip broke, but the trunk lid flew open.

Hot, acidy smoke billowed from the trunk and filled my

nose. Instantly I couldn't breathe. I reeled back, choking. The people screaming behind me were coming closer. *I'm okay!* I covered my nose with my T-shirt, gulped in a breath, and reached into the smoke, my eyes burning.

I felt around on the hot floor of the trunk . . . rough carpet, a cardboard box, and burlap. *Burlap!* I grabbed, pulled out something wide and heavy. *Shield!*

Flames roared and voices screamed, "It's going to blow!!"

"Get out of there!"

"Elijah, NO!!"

The junkyard man grabbed the back of my T-shirt and yanked. Blindly I stumbled backward and then turned and ran, my eyes and lungs scorched. People ran up to me, Skid and Rob and Skid's mom among them. The men with shovels stared at me like I was crazy.

"I got it, man! I got it!" I said.

"The shield and helmet?!" Rob gasped.

A bolt of horror shot through me. *Helmet?!*

I turned back to the burning car. Skid grabbed my arm. "You're not going—"

Boom! The ground shuddered. Flames shot out from under the car in all directions. The crowd cried out in one voice and pulled back. Yellow flames engulfed the black, brittle frame of Stan Dowland's car.

"The helmet and sword . . ." I moaned. "What if—"

Reece was beside me now. "C'mon, let's get this in the car before people start asking questions."

It was a ritual by now to take our treasure to a secret spot and examine it. We had peeked into the bag and cheered. It was a shield, all right.

"Devil's Cranium," I whispered on the way back home.

Skid swore his mom to secrecy. When she dropped us off at the Camp Mudj maintenance building, she pulled me over and said firmly, "Elijah, I'm not your mom. But here's fair warning: you pull a caper like that again, and I'll sic your mother, your father, and Dom loose on you all at once."

"I'm okay," I said.

"Then why are you covering your arm?"

I lifted my hand. The hair on my forearm was singed off, and a blister rose around a nasty-looking red patch. It stung like the dickens. "I'll put aloe on it. I'm okay."

"By the grace of God!" she barked. "That armor is important to you kids. But I will not stand by and watch my son's best friend fry himself to a crisp! I'm a mother! We have a code of ethics!"

Marcus Skidmore's best friend? Me? He told his mom I'm his best friend?! I beamed.

She slapped my shoulder with the back of her hand. "You take me serious now!"

"Yes, ma'am. It won't happen again."

"You got that right!"

The four of us loaded the golf cart with food and gear and a first-aid kit. I drove by the house to let Mom know where we were going. She met us at the door with a strange look on her face. I thought Carlotta Skidmore had already ratted on me.

"What's up?" I asked uneasily, hiding the burn.

She said, "Elijah, I need to talk to you—alone."

She knows. Carlotta snuck over here while we loaded the cart and ratted on me. This means a permanent grounding for sure.

"What'd I do?" I asked, bracing to get viped and grounded.

"It's not you, hon." She looked over my shoulder to the others. "You're in the middle of something, aren't you?"

Reece waved from the front seat of the cart and said, "It's okay. We'll wait at the lodge."

Skid drove the cart off, and I followed Mom into the formal living room where Dad always brought me for the big talks. The house was empty. A weird feeling crept over me. *What's wrong?* The nightmare of Rob's parents' near split popped into my head. I asked, "Where's Dad?"

"He's with a group of campers. Have a seat."

We sat together on the couch, my heart thumping, my mind spinning, and my arm in searing pain.

Are Mom and Dad splitting up? Or is it Francine? Did word come that she's dead? Since she was our only lead on the sword, is the trip cancelled? Or is it my Latin grade?

"It's not bad news, Elijah. It might even be good news." She took a deep breath and so did I. "You know those false walls your Uncle Dorian and Aunt Grace uncovered at The Castle a while back?"

"Yeah . . ."

"Well, Dorian found some documents in there. Papers about the history of Magdeline . . . and possible information about our biological mother."

I sat back, relieved and excited. "You know who she is?"

"Not yet. But we have something to go on for the first time in our lives. We grew up in Magdeline but never lived in that old house. We can't imagine why our family secrets were hidden behind a false wall. I haven't told the girls yet. I don't want to get their hopes up. But I thought you should know. If you catch snippets of our talking, that's what's going on." She tugged on my ear. "We can't get anything past you anyway."

She settled into the couch, curled her feet up under her, and broke into a big, shaky smile. "I've wondered about it a lot. After your Grandma Wingate passed away, I thought that was the end of it. She was the only one who knew about our biological parents. If we find out anything solid, I'll let you know. The search might take months and might involve my traveling some. That's why I'm going to Ireland. There's a woman there who may have information. We have other leads—in Scotland. But this one seems the most promising. We'll have to be patient with the process. Dorian and I have talked it over and agree that finding our mother is more important than your Aunt Grace sampling Irish teas."

Thinking about my own quest, I said, "I hear you."

"Let Dorian tell Rob in his own way."

"Sure." I heaved a sigh of relief. No bad news. And the possibility of a new grandma? Don't get me wrong, Grandma Creek was a bucket load of funny-old-person—enough for twenty kids—but it couldn't hurt to have another one.

Light mist was falling when the four of us stopped short of the summit of Devil's Cranium under a flame-red maple tree. I unloaded the pop-up tent and had it set up in a minute. "This will hold us all." We crawled in, and the red tent and leaves cast a glow over our circle of four.

Reece put on gloves and started to take the shield out of the bag. Then she stopped and sighed, "This was Mei's job. And . . . she always made the sketches too. Who's going to make sketches?"

"I will," I said.

Rob said, "Or . . . we could take pictures and mail them to Japan. She could make sketches and send them back."

Reece said, "Let's do that! Mei misses us like crazy!"

Skid said, "Not that we're ragging on your talent, Creek, but keeping Mei involved is a good idea."

Reece pulled out the shield of faith. It was about three feet across and round in shape, but the edges were angular, not curved. Rob counted the angles. "It has twelve sides."

Skid nodded. "Twelve tribes, twelve apostles."

Golden brads or knobs moved in a spiral pattern from

the outside edge to a shiny disc with gray, metal crosspieces in the center. Surrounding the disc were slashes radiating out like irregular sunbeams made of the same gray metal. The surface of the shield was pock-marked and smudged.

"It's heavy," Reece said, "definitely metal; the back is hard leather or wood."

There were two leather straps on the back, one in the middle and one on the side to hold the shield with. I stuck my arm through the bands and held it in front of me.

Skid quoted, "'Take up the shield of faith, with which you can extinguish all the flaming arrows of the evil one.'"

Noting the singed hairs on my arm, I asked, "What's that mean—'flaming arrows of the evil one'?"

Skid checked the Quella. "The commentary says they are Satan's attempts to destroy us. The point is that faith in God will stop his destroying power."

"Then . . . the . . . evil one probably doesn't like it that we have this."

We got quiet. After a minute Reece asked, "Do you see any letters?"

"Not yet," said Rob. "But they may be encrypted. The Stallards said so."

I borrowed one of Reece's gloves and ran my fingers over the shield's war scars. Black dust stained my fingertips. "This is soot. These are scorch marks."

"Here's something else," Skid said, reading from the Quella. "It's talking about our reward being kept in Heaven for . . . 'you, who through faith are shielded by God's power until the coming of the salvation that is ready to be revealed in the last time. In this you greatly rejoice, though now for a little while you may have had to suffer grief in all kinds of trials. These have come so that your faith—of greater worth than gold, which perishes even though refined by fire—may be proved genuine.'" Skid nodded. "Deep stuff."

My fingers grazed the burn bandage on my arm.

"Hey look," Reece said, "the backing is loose."

Rob said, "Be careful that it doesn't fall apart."

She gently pried the metal covering of the shield from the backing. "Elijah, do you have a flashlight?"

I dug it out of the equipment box and clicked it on.

"There's something in here," she said.

We moved in. "What is it?" Rob asked eagerly.

"Metal braces . . . and an old piece of paper!"

Even Reece's little hand wouldn't fit down into the space. It took a good twenty minutes of shaking and poking to get it out without tearing the paper. At last, it came free and dropped out.

"It's like a page from a book," Reece said.

Rob said, "English letters, but it's another language."

"Maybe it talks about faith," I said.

Rob studied it up close. "This isn't paper. It's parchment. We have to get a picture of this to the Stallards!"

Chapter 4

LATIN was a nightmare, as expressed in a poem scrawled in the back of my secondhand Latin book: *Latin is a language, as dead as dead can be. It killed all the Romans, and now it's killing me.* The problem wasn't my mind being weak on language. Basketball Mike was a brain, but he popped antacids before class every day; straight-A cheater Dora Ann dropped out after the first week. We went from being the unlucky thirteen to the twelve martyrs. But every day Rob walked by on his way to lunch, doing his hula dance and mouthing words like weeny, weedy, weeky. No matter how rotten class was, Rob's loony hula dance made it bearable.

Most days I'd recuperate from Abner's verbal lashings by running cross-country. I was the coach's favorite from day one because I could outrun everyone else and was already close to breaking the school record. It was sweet that I could chalk up all those jogs through Telanoo as "building a well-rounded academic and extracurricular portfolio." Maybe college was back on the horizon after all. Maybe I could major in roaming.

Since we couldn't get together much—what with all the portfolio building and Emma's raging curiosity—I called the Stallards myself about the shield and mentioned the idea of sending pictures to Mei. Dr. Eloise freaked. "Oh dear, you haven't done it already, have you?!"

"No," I said.

"Then don't! You shouldn't develop photos at an outside establishment. No part of the armor is to be seen by the public eye. One of you will either have to draw the shield by hand or . . . none of you have a darkroom, do you? . . . No?"

I mentioned the page we found in the shield.

"Is that so? Can you read any of the words?"

I did the best I could, and she thanked me for trying. "I've made a few notes. We'll see where this takes us."

The Stallards called back the next day. They were antsy to fly down but couldn't. "We are condensing our classes as it is to free up time for Ireland. Keep everything under wraps," she warned again.

Was it my imagination, or were the Chicago archaeologists getting more secretive and more worried about the quest?

Dr. Eloise's voice crackled through the phone, "Ah, before I forget, what have you heard from Francine Dowland?"

A lump formed in my stomach. "We can't find her."

Long pause. "Oh dear," she said darkly.

"I called and called and even asked Officer Taylor to help me," I defended. "It's like she disappeared."

There was another long pause. "We . . . we must not lose faith. Faith without works is dead, isn't it?" she said cheerily.

I'd started going to Reece's church, and nobody gave me grief over the rubber ducky caper. (I'd put revenge against Rob on hold for lack of time.) Going to church involved a lot of sitting still and listening, sort of like school. But since the teens banded together in the front center pews, I got to sit with Reece and her church friends who were mostly from other schools. All of a sudden, I had a new circle of friends.

The minister usually talked about Jesus and other Bible people and told pretty decent jokes. I always went away feeling really good on the inside, though I can't put my finger on why exactly. As Halloween approached, he started a set of sermons on the occult. He mentioned The Crystal See by name, calling it a place of deception at best, a gateway to Hell at worst. He pointed a finger down over the pulpit and warned us kids point-blank: *"Necromancy* means contacting the dead, a practice among the nations since the dawn of time. And the question we ask is, does it work or are mediums frauds?" He paused. "The Lord never said it had no power. He said don't do it. In exchange for the remote possibility that one actually can give you supernatural knowledge from beyond, you expose yourself to the influence of demons. Demons impersonate the dead to control the living and lure them away from God."

Skid had told me that the spirit world was not a safe place. A wispy chill went down my backbone. Why? I didn't know.

The minister looked at the whole congregation. "When the Lord spoke about the end of days, he said: 'At that time many will turn away from the faith and will betray and hate each other, and many false prophets will appear and deceive many people. Because of the increase of wickedness, the love of most will grow cold.' He also asked this unsettling question: 'When the Son of Man comes, will he find faith on the earth?'

"Friends, it's an ominously simple formula he gave us: no faith in Jesus, no love in the world."

Well, I hate to admit it, but that mention of The Crystal See just made me want to stop by, just to peek into the spirit world and see what it was like. All this spirit stuff was new to me, and I wanted to roam around in it.

I mentioned that to Skid the next day at my locker, and he about took my head off. "Just see how people live who believe those lies, just once, Creek. My Dad's been to West Africa where voodoo was born—saw it firsthand. It's all filth and fear." He jabbed himself in the chest, his eyes blazing. "My ancestors were stuck in it. My distant relatives still are; it's my roots. Along dirt roads you got piles of black, crusty, oozing slime where people pour blood over their gods day after day."

"Weird," I said agreeably.

"You can put a different face on it, call it fortune-telling or a séance, but it's all the same. It's like worshiping a boo hag, but there's a real entity behind it, luring you in. Once you're in, it don't want to let you out."

He was getting more like his military dad every day. I backed off. "Okay, okay. I was just saying . . ."

He cooled off and helped me shove my books into the

locker. "I'm supposed to look after you, that's all. Keep you on the straight and narrow."

By mid-October only Reece's passport hadn't come. There was still no word about Francine. But the Stallards hadn't canceled the trip, so permission was granted for us to be out of school for a week-long "educational and cultural tour of Ireland." The teachers managed to knock some wind out of our sails by assigning us homework for that week. Abner's two-page nightmare was for me to explain why the Roman hordes had or had not invaded Ireland during their conquest of the known world—in Latin, of course. How I was supposed to find this out while snooping through an old castle was beyond me. But question Miss Abner and you fry.

Reece came up to my locker by herself. I caught her shocked expression and expected the worst.

"You'll never guess! Not in a million years!"

I knew it was good news.

"Guess where Mei is!"

I looked around.

"Not here. Better! In London! She's doing a homestay to study English for six weeks!"

"That's great," I said mildly.

"Don't you get it? She can come to Ireland and go with us to look for—" she glanced around and lowered her voice, "the you-know. See how God worked it out?"

I didn't see.

"If she had stayed here in America, her parents would never have let her go with us," Reece bubbled over, "but now she can tour the British Isles with her parents' full approval because it's culture! Mom's calling the Stallards to make sure it's okay, but it will be. She's one of us again!"

"Who's one of us?" said a voice behind us.

It was Emma.

Reece was going to try to go if her passport came in time. She broke the news to Emma, who started working the possibilities over lunch. "My family travels a lot," she fished for an invitation. "I have a passport," she hinted. Even when Reece explained that it was independent study with these professors we know, Emma kept trying to worm her way in.

"It's nothing personal," I said finally. "The Stal—I mean, the professors are working with us four. And Mei. It's been planned for weeks."

"Mei? She's not even at school anymore!" Emma shot a hurt look at Reece.

Reece said apologetically, "I'm still not positive that I can go—it all depends."

Emma pouted over her food a minute. "Well, Reece," she said slowly, "if it turns out you can't go . . ." She grinned at me and fluttered her eyelashes, "I could take your place."

I swallowed hard. *Uh-oh.*

The Stallards had written to Francine Dowland but hadn't heard back. It occurred to me that she could have been lying about the sword; she might have stolen it like she did the shoes of peace and the journals. *That former preacher's wife is probably a penny-ante thief. Who's to say the sword hasn't been here all along?* But I had no proof.

Reece was praying and cranking up her therapy but was still on crutches. If she didn't go, I couldn't either. I didn't tell Emma though. Things were getting complicated. *Is God really working it out?* I wondered. *Did he let Mei's parents send her home so she could end up in England and fly over to Ireland and meet us because the sword is there? Will Reece get to go? Will we find Francine? Will she help us? Where is the sword?!*

This was the biggest thing in my life ever, but I had no control over any of it. I could hardly sleep for the tension building up in me.

In a few days I got a call from the Stallards. "It's about Francine," said Dr. Eloise.

"Did you find her?" I asked, feeling queasy.

"She was staying in Louisville with friends. She wasn't much help. To make a long story short: the Dowland family visited several castles and antique shops on their tour. Toward the end of their trip, Stan took a day for himself while Francine and their daughter Kate spent the day shopping in Dublin. He returned with the armor, saying he'd seen it in a shop and couldn't get it out of his mind."

I thought a moment. "At least we know it's a one-day drive from Dublin. That should narrow the field."

She sighed. "Ireland is small, roughly the size of Ohio."

I got it. "So you can get anywhere and back in one day?"

"Precisely."

"What do we do?" I asked, wondering how they found Francine when the Magdeline police couldn't.

"She did provide us with a list of the castles and shops."

"We have to hit 'em all?!"

"It will be grueling. Approximately a thousand miles of driving. Not a lot of time for leisurely dining and sightseeing. But if we are to find the sword . . ."

"We can do it!" I said, praying like crazy. *C'mon, please!*

"Elijah, I hesitate to ask such a personal question, but what about Reece? How will she fare?"

"She's good to go once her passport comes in," I said, faking confidence. "And you can ask her point-blank about her problem anytime. She hates it when people tiptoe around it."

"Excellent. One more point. Dale and I believe we should examine the shield before we go. We'll drive down this weekend and bring the shoes. Does your camp have a vacancy in one of the cabins?"

"I'll check. There's probably a room at the lodge."

"Any accommodation will be fine—we live simply."

The next day I was slogging down the hall toward Latin when Reece pounced on me like a cat and yanked me into a corner. In her shaking hand was a navy blue passport. "We're going!" she whispered. "We're all going to Ireland. The five of us together again! He worked it out for us, Elijah! He did it!"

A jolt of disbelief coursed through me. Reece and I stood there grinning at each other, speechless and overjoyed in our usual own private world, until I got a thick elbow in the back.

I whirled. It was that bulk Justin Brill with a slimy look on his face. "Hey, Nature Boy, I hear you got religion." He leered at Reece. "Elliston, maybe he can lay hands on you and heal you." His mocking eyes shifted to me as he lumbered off.

Chapter 5

XXXXXXXXXXXXXXXXXXXXXXXXXXXXXXXXXXXXXXXXXXXXXXXXXXXXXXXXXXX

THE day before takeoff, the Stallards arrived with the shoes of peace, which we all looked over again as if we'd never seen them. Dr. Dale had brought measuring instruments and some sort of chemicals to test the shield. We met at the lodge, lit a fire, and gathered around. When Reece brought the shield out of the sack, the Chicago archaeologists leaned over and gazed at it like it was their own new baby.

"We've been doing research based on your description," Dr. Eloise said after a minute.

Skid flipped open the Quella. "The first mention of the shield is when God told Abraham not to be afraid. He said, 'I am your shield, your very great reward.'"

Rob said, "A warrior's shield was the most important defensive piece. It protected the whole body and even the other parts of the armor."

"Correct," said Dr. Eloise.

Dr. Dale reported, "The shield is average size—around three feet across—to fit an average person, meaning the general population. Faith must fit you just like shoes or a helmet. It must be of a size you can wield, but sufficient to protect you. Not too big or too little."

"A person can have too big a faith?" Reece asked.

"There's no such thing. What I'm saying is that God will give you sufficient faith for your fiery trials."

At the words "fiery trials," the others glanced in my direction. Skid whispered "pyro" at me. I frowned back and mouthed, "Am not!"

Dr. Dale lifted the shield, looked at it sideways, and bounced it in his hands. "Approximately an inch thick around the edges, fifteen to twenty pounds." He went on as if talking to himself. "Earlier shields were edged in bronze. This one is *sheeted* in bronze, indicating a later origin."

"Or possibly a later enhancement," Dr. Eloise added.

He agreed. "The shape is more like ancient Sumerian, Assyrian—"

"Or Greek!" Rob chimed. "I've been doing my own research!"

"Excellent, Mr. Rob," chirped Dr. Eloise. "You are such a little man already!"

She meant it as a compliment, but the "little man" label deflated my short cousin. He managed a polite smile and rolled his eyes at me when they weren't looking.

Dr. Dale reported, "These steel enhancements are also later additions. These slashes could be stylized sun rays radiating from the disc—" He paused, studied them a minute. "Their irregularities seem to be a deliberate design."

Dr. Eloise agreed. "It could be our encryption."

"Now that you mention it, there seem to be six distinct patterns of rays separated by small spaces. If only we were back at our lab," he said longingly. They analyzed the lines a long time. "Nothing familiar to me," he said finally.

"Nor me," she said.

"Well, let's move ahead to the shape of the shield."

"It's twelve-sided, like the apostles!" chimed Rob.

Reece laughed. "The apostles weren't twelve-sided!"

Dr. Eloise let out a high-pitched "Skwagack!" like some prehistoric bird. We laughed at her laugh, then at each other, pretending we were still laughing at Rob, until we all were cackling. It suddenly hit us all: *we're really going! Even Mei. It's really happening. Our quest has just gone global!*

When we'd settled down, Dr. Eloise said, "We know what you mean, Rob. Back into the analysis of the shield."

Rob said, "It's curved to deflect arrows and javelins and to allow the armor bearer to rest the upper edge on his shoulder."

The Stallards were impressed. Skid got Rob in a friendly headlock. "He's our resident research-nerd-meteorologist."

"And actor," said Reece. She made an observation, "That cross in the middle. It's not like a church cross. The two sticks are the same length."

"Ah, the cross!" said Dr. Eloise. "A most ancient symbol. It predates Christianity and is evidenced in virtually every major culture. To some it meant the four directions, to others eternal life, the four winds, or four corners of the earth. Over the centuries the cross has been twisted, inverted, looped, and broken to give it some new or perverse meaning. Denominations have claimed their own designs—everyone wants to claim the cross." She leveled her eyes at us. "They know in their hearts the cross has power; some just don't understand what *kind* of power."

"Amen," I said. Dr. Eloise's mysterious comments didn't put me in the blind panic they used to.

Dr. Dale continued the analysis. "The arm and hand straps, called the porpax and antilabe, are positioned to distribute the weight. A shield should be held waist high, the forearm parallel to the ground. The curved shape is designed for pushing ahead, and these spiraled brads deflect the thrust of a blade point. Its smaller size suggests that a warrior has a better chance of survival if he stands close to another warrior. In this way each is protecting the right flank, that is, the sword arm of the other.

Reece said, "A person's faith helps his friend's."

"Yes. One disadvantage of a more cumbersome shield is that a strong wind can pull it away, throwing its wearer off balance. For a long-distance military campaign in unpredictable weather, a huge shield is not necessarily the most practical."

Reece smiled at me, "Even a little bit of faith works."

Dr. Dale put down the shield, nodding slowly. "An excellent piece of armor, the shield of faith. One caution I must mention, however." His merry mood turned quiet and intense. "Shields have been known to shatter upon impact . . . especially on the front lines . . . during the initial attack."

Only Skid nodded that he understood.

Dr. Eloise cleared her throat and smiled eagerly. "About the page you found . . ."

Reece had it in a plastic sleeve pressed between two pieces of cardboard. She handed it over to Dr. Eloise. "We never touched it with our bare hands."

"Good girl," said Dr. Eloise, and then to me, "You did an excellent job with the language on the page. After hours of research, we believe we've identified it."

It was then I realized how tired they looked. I said, "I got a really nice room for you here in the lodge. First floor."

Dr. Eloise thanked me. Dr. Dale brought a book out of his raggedy briefcase and opened it. They compared the page with pictures in the book. Dr. Eloise's hand slowly went to her mouth in amazement. "Will wonders never cease . . ."

"What is it?" I asked.

"It does appear to be a lost page from the most ancient manuscript in Ireland . . . a book called the *Cathach,* which means 'warrior.' If this is genuine . . ."

As if cued by the same director, the Stallards suddenly looked at each other long and hard. Dr. Dale said, "Hmm. This is at once a blessing and a complication. We must be cautious, for now we venture into another area of antiquities. A cutthroat business." He studied the page in his wife's hand. "But this could possibly lead us to the sword."

"Where is the book it came from?" Rob asked.

"In Dublin." She turned to Dr. Dale. "We'll need to acquire special permission."

"We have no time," he said with concern. "Perhaps a phone call of introduction before we simply appear at their door and ask to see the manuscript."

"What kind of manuscript?" I asked.

"It's a portion of the book of Psalms."

"Oh." Disappointment showed in my voice.

Dr. Eloise smiled tolerantly. "Yes, yes, just a book of dusty old poems, you're thinking. But these poems were transcribed by a spiritual warrior named Columba who risked his life to keep them. They have been used for warfare for centuries! I believe it's no coincidence that this book is stored in the very city already on our itinerary." Dr. Eloise closed her eyes. "Psalm 3:3: 'You are a shield around me.' Psalm 7:10: 'My shield is God Most High.' Psalm 33:20: 'We wait in hope for the LORD; he is our help and our shield.'" She smiled. "Words from the *Warrior*."

Skid said, "Preach on, sista!"

The shield was returned to its burlap bag. "Where is it to be stored?" Dr. Eloise asked.

Rob said, "In my attic. We had the armor at Reece's until our remodeling was done."

"We shall need to take the page to Ireland." Her eyes sparkled with wonder. "Thank you, children. This is the most exciting venture of our lives. We deeply appreciate you. Well," she stood, "we must hit the proverbial hay.

Tomorrow: Ireland! Logistics have been discussed with your parents. And one more thing: if you have not prepared your heart, do so before departure."

"What do you mean?" I asked.

"It's particularly important that we keep perspective during this season of pagan Celtic festivals. In Ireland the holiday of Halloween is called *Samhain.* On this night the pagans say that the veil between the worlds grows thin. I don't expect trouble, but we are on a spiritual quest. So pray," was her answer. "Pray hard."

I was too excited to sleep. Mom was up too, making meals ahead for Dad and the twins.

"I'm going for a walk, Mom."

"It's midnight, and you're in your jammies."

"I'll change."

"Where are you going?"

"Owl Woods, maybe farther. Cross-country training."

"In the middle of the night? My, such a disciplined son I have!" she kidded. "Take your flashlight."

"There's a gibbous moon."

"Whatever. Be back soon."

I ran full tilt for over half an hour and ended up due west of Devil's Cranium in a big gully lined with smooth, stone walls and steep, dirt banks. I sat under a huge slab overhang. The moon broke over the hill and sparkled on a narrow, trickling stream at my feet. *El-Telan-Yah?*

Quiet settled over me—the Presence.

Thank you, I said with a knot in my chest. *Thanks for letting Reece go so I could go . . . You are letting her, aren't you? She's not having a relapse tonight, I hope. Because I made a deal: I can't go if she doesn't. And thanks for working it out so Mei could come . . . the long way around the earth. Did you really work all that out? Because that's really planning ahead.*

Sitting there in the moonlit dark, I felt as far from tomorrow as a person could. It wasn't real. *I hate to bother you, but it's just one little thing: could you lead us to the sword? We have no clues, so we're counting on you.*

What was to be my final purpose in finding the whole armor? I mulled over the professors' words and wondered, *If this is war, who's the enemy exactly? Who am I fighting?* I yearned to own a Quella. *One more thing, God. It would be handy to have a Bible where I can find things quick.*

The trickling stream like a ribbon of light led me deeper into the unexplored part of Telanoo. *If you want me to fight, I want to know my enemy. I want to see him. I mean it. I'm not just some kid fooling around with my beliefs, God.* Leaves fell around me like tiptoes. *I'm ready to go with the belt of truth and the shoes of peace, and now the shield of faith. I believe in you. I said so in front of a church. I've been baptized. You've washed away my sins. I'm caught up, right?* Cautiously I demanded, *So show me who I'm fighting against.*

All right.

His answer had a stern, deep ring. A ferocious shiver ran through me. What had I just asked for?

Chapter 6

✳✳✳

EVERYONE met at my house the next day. Reece was the last to arrive. I don't mind saying that I was on pins and needles until her mom's car pulled up. She was shaky but used only a cane. I heaved a huge sigh of relief.

Lots of hugs went around, all the parents squeezing everybody else's kids and crying over their own. Mom and Dad kissed a long time; then we loaded into the camp van, and Uncle Dorian drove us to Port Columbus International Airport.

The Stallards got us checked in, and Dr. Dale handed out cloth envelopes on cords to hang around our necks. "You are to wear these travel packs hidden on your person at all times. Each packet contains a miniature map of Ireland that shows the locations we'll be investigating, plus contact names and phone numbers in case we get separated." He handed a card to Dorian. "You'll notice an addition to our itinerary."

Uncle Dorian looked at the card darkly. "Grafton Institute. What's there?"

"A book we must see." Dr. Eloise went on with the instructions. "In your packs you'll also find a little Irish currency: change for the phone or emergency fare. After losing our daughter on several occasions, we've come up with this plan. It saves time backtracking."

We said good-bye to Uncle Dorian, breezed through security, and boarded. Mom sat between Skid and Reece on the three-seat side of the plane; Rob was in front of them with Dr. Eloise and a really big lady. I sat across the aisle next to the window with Dr. Dale. The plane started to taxi.

A strange, dark fear crept into me. "We're going."

"Are you afraid of flying?" he asked.

The plane gained momentum, roaring and rattling. My fingers gripped the armrests. "No, but—"

"It's the lack of control we feel," he consoled me. "Eloise used to hate flying until she understood that she was simply afraid of dying." He shook his head at me as if that were silly. "Now before we fly, she simply plans on dying. She makes sure that everything is in order and spends the night in prayer—confessing her sins and seeking peace. Ever since she discovered this method, she's able to set off into the wild, blue yonder happy as one could be!"

I glanced over at Dr. Eloise. She was talking the ears off Rob and the big lady.

"When one feels out of control, Elijah, one must *not* fight it but determine to move through fear to courage." Dr. Dale looked at me directly. "Move toward your destiny, Elijah. If you retreat from it, you are beaten."

I wasn't into talking death while we hurtled along the runway at two hundred miles an hour. So I nodded and glanced out the window as the ground dropped out from under me. Across the aisle and back one seat, Skid—Mr.

Height Fright—was into his Quella, probably reading up on Heaven. My mom—sort of white-knuckled herself—was giving him a mommy talk.

"Hey, Skidmore," I called back, "here's good advice: if you just *plan* on crashing and dying, you'll feel a lot better."

If looks could kill, I'd have been dead. Mom wasn't thrilled over my advice either.

Dr. Dale smiled a sleepy smile. "We're all in God's hands."

I leaned my head back—the plane zoomed up, up, up and then leveled off while my stomach kept going up another hundred feet. The captain gave us the weather and time of arrival in Boston where we'd switch planes for Ireland.

Dr. Dale pulled out a flask, the kind people keep whiskey in. "Coffee," he said and took a sip.

I got a whiff, or I'm not sure I would have believed him.

Earth dropped away. We angled up into the clouds. The outside world was nothing to me but a big silver wing cutting through blinding whiteness until the sun burst through.

"Thunderheads, children!" Dr. Eloise chirped.

The patchwork fields of central Ohio were gone, and the new landscape was miles and miles of clouds and light. I whispered to myself, "God's hands."

Once in Boston and waiting for our flight out, we sat at the gate with all kinds of people who spoke with Irish brogues. *This is really happening. We're really going!* We got snacks, and Dr. Dale refilled his coffee flask. The sun sank toward the horizon as we boarded. This time we all were on the same side of a much bigger plane.

In no time we were high over Boston at twilight. "The street lights!" Reece said, poking me between the seats. "They look like fairy trails!"

By the time we passed over Maine, the world had gone dark. Again I sat in the window seat over a massive wing, its silver blade taking swipes at the full moon. Mom drifted off when we passed over Newfoundland, so Dr. Dale lectured me about the first explorers to America. "The very first settlers were Indians, as we call them. But evidence is emerging in texts and artifacts that lends support to the theory that Christopher Columbus was not the first European discoverer. One of the first explorers may have been Brendan the Navigator."

"Never heard of him," I said.

"He was one of a number of Irish who called themselves the *peregrini*—Brendan, Patrick, Columba, and others— wanderers for the faith who set out like Abraham, not knowing where God would lead but willing to go nonetheless."

"*Peregrini?*"

"You've heard of peregrine falcons?"

"Fastest birds on the planet."

"It's from the same root word, meaning 'pilgrim.'"

Suddenly he nodded off. Just as I started to think he'd stopped breathing, the dignified Dr. Dale began snoring like an outboard motor and didn't let up until the meal came. As we dug into our little dinners, he leaned over. "Eloise has been having dreams."

This got my attention because of my dream about the fire. "What kind of dreams?"

"She sees ancient standing stones holding hands and crying out. She can't understand what they are saying. You are leading us through the stones, and then we are on a high hill."

"What's it mean?" I asked.

"We don't put too much stock in dreams, Elijah. One never wants to sink into divination. But occasionally they teach us about Scripture or show us an aspect about ourselves we need to face. In the last days there will be a resurgence of visions and dreams. But dreams are never the final word."

We got up and stretched. Reece asked to borrow my seat near the window. We moved down and Mom moved back a row. I told Reece, "It's dark out now, but you can have my seat the rest of the way and be the first to see Ireland."

Dr. Dale nodded off again; things got quiet. Reece turned to me and said bluntly, "Emma likes you."

It was too close quarters for a discussion like this. "So?"

"I wanted you to know that if . . . if you wanted to like her back . . . I'd still . . . we'd still be friends, I hope. Forever."

There was silence until I muttered, "She's out of the loop."

"What loop?" Reece asked.

"The armor loop, the clan loop, any loop you're talking about." I yanked the flight magazine out of the seat pocket and flipped through it. "She's in the lunch loop—that's *all.*"

"Okay. That's . . . good." She turned to stare out the dark window, and I caught a glimpse of her smiling reflection.

Everyone took turns catnapping until hours later when we had breakfast. Dr. Dale and I made small talk. He looked at his watch and beamed. "One hour. I've waited years for this."

I was stunned. "You mean you've been looking for the armor of God since before you met us?"

"Oh yes." He paused, took a sip of coffee, and held it in his mouth for a second. His Adam's apple bobbed as the coffee went down. "Many's the year."

I wasn't sure how to feel about that. It put him more in Dowland's court: an old guy who'd made armor-hunting his life's work.

"Why do you think I—I mean *we* found it?" I asked.

He scratched his stubbly chin. "It appears that the Lord has been preparing you for leadership since your birth. As the eldest child you are called upon to care for the twins. You've spent much time in the wilderness, like Moses, Paul, and the prophet Elijah himself, who came from obscurity and appeared on the scene a full-fledged messenger of the

Lord. There are many striking similarities. And your faith is not an inherited one. You have reasoned it out yourself. Rather uncanny."

"Do you think I'm the old Elijah reincarnated?"

Dr. Dale sighed tiredly. "Son, we must have some long theological talks very soon! At this point in your life—on the cusp of adulthood and possibly a mission for which you are completely unprepared—you must be extremely careful to listen to the right voices. We would not want your little craft set adrift on the sea of life only to be immediately blown off course by ill winds, the foul storms of the evil one."

"Yeah, but . . . don't the winds and waves obey God?" I was remembering the tornado and the big kahuna wave.

He took a slug from his coffee flask and nodded. "I'm speaking in metaphors—the ill winds of ignorance, the storms of life, the dark clouds of uncertainty."

In one haggard, pasty-mouthed clump, we de-boarded at Shannon International Airport. Skid was wrung out, and Mom got a sudden case of the jitters about searching for her mother by herself. We made it through customs and changed our American cash to Irish. As the sun came up, we loaded our stuff into a rental van, and Dr. Eloise flashed around an Irish newspaper with a weather photo on the front page. "We've lost a night's sleep, and a terrible storm is on its way. The rental agent warned us of possible heavy rains with winds of up to fifty miles an hour. But we may be able to outrun the worst of it if we hurry."

Rob was the first to notice that the steering wheel was on the right side of the car. He watched Dr. Dale buckle himself into the driver's seat. "Do you know how to drive on the right side of the car on the left side of the road?"

"Mm-hmm," he mumbled distractedly, trying his hands on the gearshift and steering wheel. "It's those blasted roundabouts." He turned on the ignition and said to Mom, "Jodi, are we to drop you off at a designated spot?"

Mom gave him a map. "Right there. I've marked the route in red. My contact is meeting us at the mouth of the Shannon River. Her name's Ruthie. She lives where . . . my mother use to live. If the gate's not open, we're supposed to call."

Eloise made us all bow our heads. She prayed for Mom to find success and peace and for us all to be safe on our adventure. "And finally, O Most High," she prayed, "as this most pagan holiday approaches, deliver us from the evil one!"

Dr. Dale pulled out of the airport parking lot, muttering nervously to himself, "Stay to the left, the left . . . left."

The storm blew in as we headed out. Through sheets of pelting rain, Ireland looked similar to Ohio: smooth hills, lots of farms, trees turning orange and yellow. But there were sheep farms everywhere, surrounded by stone fences; and when we went through our first village, it was clear we weren't in Ohio. Stores of all different colors edged right up to the street, with names like Jonah Rylee's Pub and Brian Spellissy's Books. The village streets were narrow and winding. But the biggest shocks were the remains of castles perched on lonely hills.

Dr. Dale was right about the roundabouts. You'd careen into the circle of highway going fifty—on the left side, hopefully—and keep going around until you found the right road. Then you'd shoot off with cars coming at you and cars beside you. We guys thought the roundabouts were cool, but Dr. Dale sweated bullets every time he saw a sign for one ahead.

Dr. Eloise tried to navigate and give a tour at the same time. "We're on N18—these ruins, children, are anywhere from—watch for signs for N69, dear—two hundred to— that's N21, we don't want that—put the wipers on high. I can't see a thing in this torrent—take the left lane. No, it's the right—one thousand years old!" She patted Dr. Dale's arm excitedly, "We must take a few hours—there it is, N69—to visit Newgrange, which is possibly the oldest man-made—oh, look out!—man-made structure in the world, predating even the pyramids. And the Hill of Slane. Dale, we must not miss that." She leaned to her husband and whispered, "I think that hill is the one in my dream. There was a picture in the flight magazine." She turned back to us. "You children will find it very compelling, especially you, Elijah."

Mom spotted a road sign for Limerick through the torrent pounding the windshield and said cheerily, as if to calm her own nerves, "How about you kids making up limericks about Ireland? You can tell them to me when I see you again. Elijah, be sure to call me in the next day or two, so I know where to meet up." She looked at her map. "Okay, we're getting close. It will be a one-lane road. There, there it is to the left."

Suddenly we were driving down a dirt road on a narrow spit of land with angry waves crashing on either side. Mom said shakily, "This is the only road in or out. Ruthie warned me that if we came during high tide and rough seas, the road might not be passable. The address is Seven Avon Place."

The storm worsened. Windshield wipers swished frantically. Everyone peered silently ahead as waves splashed over the road. The drive ended in thick, gray woods with two big, iron gates—one open, one locked. There wasn't a number or a house visible, just two overgrown roads disappearing into the trees. "Let's try the open gate," Mom said.

A tunnel of trees swayed overhead as if it would topple on us. When Seven Avon Place came into view, everyone went stone quiet. Before us stood the spookiest place I'd ever seen. It was a massive three stories of square stone under a low roof in a bare, muddy field. Tiny, dark windows sat in rows like strange eyes. The upper windows were barred.

"Is that . . . it?" Rob broke the silence.

"Maybe it was the locked gate," Reece said encouragingly. "We should go back and try that one."

Mom looked at her notes. "Ruthie said it was a three-story, gray, stone building with small windows."

"There's no car," I said hopefully. "This has to be wrong."

Looking concerned, Dr. Eloise said to her husband, "Drive around to the back, dear. If the cars aren't parked there, we'll try the other gate."

Behind the house a bare lot spread out to other big, drab, square buildings. A little green car was parked behind the house next to a greenhouse in ruins. Mom couldn't hide her shock and whispered to herself, "My mother lived . . . here?"

We drove back around front. All the windows in the house were dark except for one faint light in the top left window. Mom looked at her watch. "Ruthie said she'd be home."

Bracing into the wind, she got out, ran up to the door, and knocked. We all waited. No one came. She dashed around back and out of sight. While she was gone, a really tall guy opened the front door and eyed us suspiciously.

"That's not Ruthie," said Rob in a sinister tone.

"We're not leaving her here," I said protectively as I jumped out of the van into the storm.

Just as Mom came back around the building, a woman appeared at the front door. She was young and tall and had a baby in her arms. As I stood by the van shivering, Mom went up the steps. They shook hands and talked a minute.

She ran back for her luggage, trembling.

"Are you sure you're going to be okay?" I asked.

"I'll be fine," she said and bit her lip. "I have to do this. Dorian's counting on me." She gave me a big, quick hug. "I'll see you in a few days," she said. "I love you."

"Love you too, Mom. Be careful."

When the door to Seven Avon Place closed, we pulled out. A horrible feeling swept through me. I wanted to jump out, go back, and protect my mom—but from what, I didn't know.

Chapter 7

WE drove out to the main highway and headed toward Ballymeade. Dr. Dale said, "If anyone asks about the nature of the trip, let's call it 'independent study.'" He added sternly, "We are here to gather information, not to dispense it."

Dr. Eloise turned to Reece cheerfully. "And Mei is still meeting us?"

Reece grinned. "She called. She and her friend are flying over from London. They'll meet us at the castle."

Dr. Eloise cleared her throat, her eyes wide and worried. "Her . . . friend is coming with us?"

Reece said, "I don't think so. She's going to some big celebration; I'm not sure what."

Dr. Eloise scanned the countryside through the side window. "I wonder what Mei has told her host family about the purpose of her trip."

Reece said blankly, "I don't know."

A quarter mile before Dr. Dale pulled into the parking lot of Ballymeade Castle, we saw its four towers poking up through the trees. Dr. Eloise was thrilled. "I hope *everyone* enjoys history!"

Skid slid me a bored look. "Woohoo."

"Behind the castle is an authentic reproduction of an Irish village. Look for opportunities to ask questions. We are in essence retracing the steps of the Dowlands in hope of finding where the armor was purchased."

We headed for the gift shop to buy tickets.

Rob asked, "What kind of sword are we looking for?"

Dr. Dale said, "The Greek word in the Ephesians passage is *machaira*: a short sword, dagger, or saber—the type Roman guards would carry. But in the book of Revelation, *rhomphaia* is used, which is a larger brandishing weapon."

Skid whipped out his Quella. "'These are the words of him who has the sharp, double-edged sword. I know where you live—where Satan has his throne. . . . Repent therefore! Otherwise, I will soon come to you and will fight against them with the sword of my mouth.'"

Dr. Eloise nodded. "Christ was speaking to the people of Pergamum, a town in modern-day Turkey. The throne of Satan at that time was either the temple of the serpent cult of Asklepios or the altar to the god Zeus. That altar, by the way, still exists and is on display in the Berlin Museum." She sighed happily. "Perhaps on our next journey, we'll go see the throne of Satan. Would you like that?"

Skid said, "Ditto on that 'woohoo.'"

Answering our creeped-out looks, she said, "Oh, sillies, it's a piece of rock in a dusty, old museum. Its power has been transferred to other sites on the planet."

"Like where?" asked Rob worriedly.

"Another day," she said evasively. "The evil one is always on the move. Now, keep your eyes open for a small, dagger-type weapon or a hefty broad-bladed sword."

"How will we know if it's *the* sword?" Rob asked.

Dr. Eloise stopped at the gift shop door. "We'll know."

Dr. Dale reminded us quietly, "We go in as tourists. One on a quest never wants to appear too eager. Take note of weapons mounted on walls or in display cases. Often history is woven or carved into a room, so look for illustrations in tapestry, furniture, and architectural details. At a time when many people didn't read, tapestries and stained glass were often used as giant storybooks for the illiterate."

We got a map of the castle layout and were let loose. Each of the towers was a stack of big rooms where lords and ladies had lived. The center of the square castle was the Great Hall. Below it was a big room called the Main Guard where soldiers used to hang out. Reece didn't want to climb the steep, circular steps in all four towers, so I offered to scout out each tower and let her know the best rooms to see.

"I'll look around here in the Great Hall," she said. "You guys can report back to me."

Before we split up, a guide came in—a little bald man with a thick accent, a brown suit, and shined-up shoes. "Did you notice the steps wind up steeply clockwise?" he asked. "That is so the enemy could not climb them and have his sword at the ready. One must use the handrail, ya see— quite the clever safety measure. If anyone has questions—"

"Swords?" I said. "Do you have swords on display?"

"In the Great Hall is mounted the Sword of Estate,

symbolizing the lord's authority to sit in judgment."

I ran to the far end of the hall, eager to see the Sword of Estate but was frankly disappointed. It was long and plain and slightly bent. I ran back to the guide. "Where did they come from, and which one's the oldest?"

Skid gave me a cool-it-Creek-don't-blow-your-cover look. The others split up while the guide showed me the duke's quarters. The sword hanging on the wall was not double-edged or dagger-like or glittering. The guide wouldn't even let me touch it.

Reece was studying the stained glass windows. On three of the walls hung huge rugs so faded I could hardly make out details. "What about those tapestries?" I asked.

"We have several." He went off on his canned speech. "And that one, the oldest in the collection, shows Jacob's dream. The story is biblical, but the art style is medieval."

I studied the tapestry. Beside the man sleeping on the ground stood a faded horse and a rider wearing armor. Even in the dreary light of the castle, I recognized a familiar twelve-sided shield with a cross in the middle. It took every ounce of willpower to stay calm. "Sir, what's the story behind the tapestry? Where'd it come from?"

"Ah, this work was created for the infamous MacMerrits —a bloody lot they were! Their history begins at Dunluce on the northern coast. The castle is not restored as this one is," he said proudly. "Dunluce has fallen into ruin. But what an impressive ruin it is. Do you plan to visit it?"

"Tomorrow!" Reece said, reading the itinerary from her travel pack.

I gave her the warning eye. *Don't give out information.* I ditched the tour guide and went hunting for the Stallards who were on top of the west battlement. I led them back down to the Great Hall. "Isn't that the shield?"

Dr. Eloise dug in her bag and brought out a tiny pair of gold binoculars mounted on a stick. "Not ordinary opera glasses," she said to me slyly. "I've had these . . . enhanced."

Flash photography was prohibited, so Dr. Dale used a little spy-looking camera to get shots of the tapestry. Rob was in awe. "We've only been here a few hours, and we have a solid lead on the armor!"

Dr. Eloise folded up her opera glasses. "The aging and damage is severe. I can see no detail on the helmet or sword. It does look like our shield though. Good work, Elijah."

I said to Reece, "Wanna see a tower? I think you'll like the south one best. It has a duchess room and clothes hanging on the wall. We'll go all the way up to the battlement and watch for Mei—if it quits storming."

Being in a real castle was cool, but I can vouch that it's no great place to live: it's cold and dark, and you could break your neck on those narrow, slippery steps.

We watched for Mei from the tower. When Reece started worrying, we went down to the gift shop and found the rest milling around, sampling blackberry jam. Rob was sniffing out teas for his mom.

"What kind of school assignments do you have to complete?" Dr. Eloise asked to pass the time.

"Photo journal for the school paper," Rob said. "And I want to learn Irish brogue—jes' far me own self."

"Travel article for social studies," Skid answered.

Reece beamed. "Oral report for speech. I don't even have to write it. But I'm keeping a journal for my Devo club."

"Oh, eeeeeeasy," said Dr. Eloise. "They'll write themselves!"

I grumbled, "Mine's on why the Roman hordes did or didn't invade Ireland, and it has to be in Latin."

Dr. Eloise's hand went to her mouth. "Oh! Dear me!" She backed away with a whimper of sympathy and wandered toward the dungeon.

We strolled the path through the folk village, posing in front of thatch-roofed houses and acting medieval for Rob's camera. That's when I spotted two dark-haired girls walking the path toward us. "Mei!" I called.

Her face lit up. She ran full force to Reece. They hugged and cried themselves silly. The next thing I knew, the five of us were in a circle, jumping and acting like girls. But I don't mind saying I felt proud—my clan was together again.

Mei introduced her friend, a pretty, medium-size girl with a serious face and light hazel eyes. "This is Sahara Dahlman." We all said hello. "She is here for a festival." They smiled at each other. Then Mei said, "It's like our festivals in Japan."

With a cool British accent, Sahara said, "It's the druid holiday of *Samhain,* what Americans call Halloween. We fly over every year to celebrate . . . the goddess." She glanced uneasily at Reece. I got the idea Sahara and Mei had been talking about Reece's religion—and maybe even the quest.

The Stallards' smiles froze on their faces. "How interesting," Dr. Dale said. "Well, is anyone hungry? Our body clocks are out of kilter. Please join us for a meal, Sahara."

"Thanks, but Mum's waiting for me in the car. We're needing to be off to the Hill of Ward for the festival."

The girls arranged to meet up with Sahara after her festival.

We went into the town to a coffee shop the professors described as "just darling" and got caught up with Mei. Dr. Eloise wanted to know about Sahara's holiday.

"She will dance in a play about the myth of the Irish sun goddess. The actors light a fire on the hill and dance around it. *Samhain* is like our *Obon* festival in Japan, when the spirits of the dead return. Sahara's mother says the walls between the worlds grow very thin on the Hill of Ward. Halloween was born there." Mei took her teacup in both hands, looking embarrassed. She said shyly to Reece, "I have learned many things about religions this year. I don't know what to believe. Sahara's religion is very much like the one in Japan."

Dr. Dale asked cautiously, "Does your friend know why we have come to Ireland?"

Mei answered, "I just told her we are searching for an ancient sword. I told her I'd see my best friends, and we would visit a castle." She looked like she was wrestling with something but couldn't get it out.

"What is it, dear?" Dr. Dale encouraged.

"Maybe it doesn't matter, but when I explained about the sword, Sahara's mother told me a story about long ago, that the druid father of the goddess began to worry when belief in Jesus came to Ireland. He told her to go throughout the world and collect all the mysteries and magics and to hide them so the Christians could never find them. I am sorry, but I think maybe the sword might be hidden forever."

Dr. Eloise said lightly, "Take care what you believe, children. Take great care, for you see every region has its tales. Is it a coincidence that many tell of sacred swords? Britain had Excalibur. Japan had the sword of Atsuta. And Ireland tells of a sword coming from afar. Cut through the fairy tales, children, and you will find their origin."

I said, "The sword of the Lord from the Garden of Eden?"

She nodded mysteriously, then steered the conversation to chitchat where I lost track. Dr. Dale was looking long and hard at his half-eaten salad. Then he put down his fork. It was the last bite of solid food he took for the next week.

Chapter 8

MEI bought postcards to make a scrapbook of Ireland. Rob offered to share the pictures from his photo journal. Then we piled into the van and headed north.

Skid asked, "Aizawa, are you still obsessed with driving?"

"Oh yes!" she said. "When I graduate, I will come back to America and get my license. Then I will drive and drive!"

Reece chirped, "We'll drive across America!"

To pass the time, we started collecting funny traffic sign sayings: "Traffic Calming" meant merge. "Soft Verge" meant to stay on the pavement and not pull off. "Don't Rubbish the Tipp" meant don't litter in Tipperary County. It was great being together again, just like the good old days.

Around noon we stopped to stretch our legs and see some famous scenery: the Cliffs of Morte. We walked up a smooth path toward a gap in a wide, *U*-shaped hill with an old castle-type watchtower up to our right at the highest point and massive knolls up to the left. As we approached the overlook, sheer cliffs stood in ranks and receded out toward the horizon. Round and green on top, they suddenly dropped off hundreds of feet straight down to churning waves and jagged rocks.

Skid's face went slack. "Oh man . . ." He fell back a step. "Whoa . . . whoa."

I answered Dr. Eloise's curious look with, "He's afraid of heights."

"Perhaps he should wait in the car," she said.

"No!" he said abruptly, fixing his eyes on those terrifying cliffs. "You guys go on," he said. After some useless pleading, Reece and Rob and Mei set off for the overlook.

"It was after Dowland's dog attacked us," I explained to Dr. Eloise. "That's when he caught height fright."

She came between Skid and his view of the cliff. "You came face-to-face with your mortality that day, didn't you? Some fear is reasonable, Marcus; we have to respect danger. But phobias are from the evil one; they keep you from optimum functioning. This is an unreasonable fear, Marcus. You can't possibly fall from here. The edge is yards away. See those slabs of stone leaning against the dirt bank, forming a waist-high barrier?" She pointed to the overlook. "See that wall of dirt and stone between you and the edge? There is *no real danger.*"

He looked over her shoulder to the cliffs for a long time, fighting for air. I waited to see what he would do.

"The evil one would love to paralyze you, Marcus," Dr. Eloise said patiently.

He breathed hard. "I need some time. You go on."

We left Skid and went to the main overlook to enjoy the view. Dr. Dale gave us a lecture on Ireland's unusual geography: "Unlike most islands, Ireland is lower in the center and higher around the edges, rimmed in many places with such cliffs. These are perhaps the most spectacular."

We went back to check on Skid; he was eyeing a break in the fence and a path that led down to a big, rock ledge with no rail. Three men in orange suits were hanging onto each other's sleeves and peering over the edge to the sea below. A sign on the fence read "Danger." Obviously, a lot of people couldn't resist the urge to go look straight down.

"Oh, dear Heaven!" said Dr. Eloise again.

"What?" I asked.

"Did you see the car in the parking lot with "Guarda" written on the side? Those are Irish policemen. These cliffs have a bad reputation for claiming lives," she paused to smile at Skid, "of those careless enough to hazard a stroll over to that edge. Winds from the Atlantic can be fierce and unpredictable, occasionally strong enough to blow stones from the sea to the top of the cliff."

A policeman walked past us. I asked what happened.

He shook his head sadly. "Poor bloke got off the tour bus, walked over for a look-see, and was gone. Fifth one this year." He eyed the swift, gray sky. "Frightful stiff wind a moment ago, still as death now. Puts the fear of God in ya sideways, don't it? Stay this side of the fence, folks."

He turned to go and then nodded to Skid and me. "But if ya venture out there to get a straight-down look like so many do, stay on yer bellies, lads, and mind the wind."

Everyone but Skid went up to the observation tower. I half expected another topography lesson from Dr. Dale, but his crinkly eyes were focused on Skid, who looked small and lonely. Under his breath Dr. Dale said, "'My enemy will say, "I have overcome him," and my foes will rejoice when I fall.'"

"What's that from?" I asked.

He seemed startled that I'd overheard him. "Words from the *Warrior,*" he answered quietly. "Do you feel it? Do you feel the darkness falling?"

His question set me back.

"He wants one of us," Dr. Dale said quietly, as if he were listening to someone.

"Who wants who?" I asked.

"The evil one, and . . . I don't know."

I looked out over the dark sea churning below us. It was a little eerie, but nothing more. I didn't feel darkness falling.

Dr. Dale wanted to stay up there awhile longer. When we came back down, Skid had passed through the break in the fence but was clinging to the post for dear life.

"What are you doing!?" Reece screamed at him.

"I'm done with it," he said. "I'm done."

"Done with what?" she demanded to know.

"His fear of heights," I answered for him.

"What's he going to do, Elijah?" Reece cried, then to Skid, "Someone just died on that ledge!"

Dr. Eloise calmly watched.

Reece threw her a glare. "You're not going to stop him?!"

Dr. Eloise called, "Marcus, it's obviously safe to crawl to the edge and look down." She turned to us. "Why don't you join him?"

Reece grabbed my arm. "No, Elijah!"

Dr. Eloise said calmly, "You must learn the difference between realistic and imagined danger. If you crawl out to the edge, you are safe. If you walk out, you are not."

We swapped glances. *Should we?* I wondered.

Skid closed his eyes and gulped. "I have to conquer this."

Mei said, "We can't let him go alone."

I looked at Rob. He bit his lip. "Good chance to experience coastal wind patterns."

"Okay," I said. "Let's do it."

Skid was gripping the fence, his eyes glued to the rim of the cliff. We made him let go and join hands.

Dr. Eloise said, "You can walk out for six paces—no more. Follow my instructions precisely, children!"

In a straight line, we counted off our steps: one, two, three, four, five, six. Reece tossed her cane aside. Mei and I helped her down, and then we crawled on our bellies. Skid was almost to the edge when his head dropped down on his arm, his lungs heaving for air. Mei scooted up and put her arm around him. "You can do it, Skid! We'll go with you."

"You're safe on your belly," Reece said. "We're safe."

He rose up on his forearms and dragged himself forward inch by inch, his legs useless behind him. "I gotta do this . . . do this." A yard from the edge, his head dropped again.

"Fear not!" Dr. Eloise called from the safety of the fence, her words almost lost in the ocean wind blast.

I pulled myself to the edge and looked down. "Wow, Skid, it's great!" Dark waves came in huge swells, turning white as they crashed over rocks and broke into fierce, white foam. It made us dizzy to watch. If someone had fallen just moments ago, his body had already washed out to sea.

I yelled over the wind, "The ocean waves are rolling in slow motion, Skid! Birds are flying underneath us! It's great! It's awesome! You'll regret it if you don't have a look!"

"A few more inches, Skid," Reece said. "You're so close!"

"We're together," Mei said.

"Be a man," Rob joked.

Skid dragged himself the last few inches, got his head over the ledge, looked down, and made a sound like he'd been punched in the gut.

"Isn't it beautiful?" Reece cried. "See the white birds against the dark-green water? Isn't God amazing?"

Dr. Eloise called, "Marcus! You did it!"

He breathed hard and said reverently, "It is awesome." Between gulps of air, he started to smile. "Whoa, baby!"

"Cured?" I asked with a grin.

Hypnotized by the swirling water and swooping birds, he murmured, "This is seriously cool."

"Time to go!" Dr. Eloise called.

We rolled over, sat up, and scooted a few yards away from the edge. The air suddenly went calm, as if the trial was over. When I judged it was safe, I stood up to dust the dirt off. The others followed.

"Oh, quickly now!" Dr. Eloise said frantically.

I'd taken a step toward Dr. Eloise when I heard a *whoosh* and saw her pitch toward us. She grabbed the fence to catch herself. The wind had changed course.

I had no time to yell for everyone to drop before the blast slammed into us. It threw me back a step. I knew I was okay, and Rob and Skid were safely between me and the fence, but . . . *Mei! Reece!!* I spun around toward the cliff.

The blast had blown Mei backward a few feet and sat her down hard. But Reece had turned for one last look at the cliffs; the wind hit her full force in the back. Already unsteady without her cane, she stumbled forward. I bolted for her. Suddenly I was looking down, my toe over the edge, the angles of the cliff telescoping below me and vanishing in dark-green swirls. My fingers clamped like iron onto Reece's arm. *We're going over. Together, headlong, the wind slamming our faces. Birds screech and bank out of our way . . .*

I saw whirlpools rising toward us as we plummeted. I saw it as if it were really happening. Behind me Dr. Eloise shrieked. I threw myself backward, pulling Reece with me—the wind fighting me for her. I spun her around and shoved her toward Rob. For a second I faced the wind and the horrified faces of Mei, Skid, and Dr. Eloise. I tottered back; my heel pressed down over nothing. Then I felt rock under my foot where there was no rock. Somehow I found

the strength to fall forward onto my knees. I scrambled
on all fours away from the ledge. We all rushed back to
Dr. Eloise; her face was a pale mask of terror. When we'd
gathered on the safe side of the fence, Reece flew into my
arms and cried.

Dr. Eloise hugged Reece long and hard and whispered
comfortingly to her. "Hot chocolate for everyone," she said
to the rest of us. "We're all right. Elijah, if you'll run up to
the tower and get Dale, we'll all get off this cliff."

We crowded around a table in the cozy Cliffs of Morte
Snack Shop. Celtic flute music played in the background
while souvenir shoppers milled around. Dr. Eloise broke the
news to her husband. He listened without batting an eye,
and his words from the *Warrior* came back to haunt me.

Trying to be jovial, Rob said, "We should add one more
rule to Skid's dad's life lessons. Lesson Nine: When it's not
safe to walk, crawl!"

Skid made lame jokes about being cured, and Mei kept
asking Reece if she was *daijoubu*. Reece sat beside me and
wouldn't let go of my arm. She, the mouth of the group—
Miss Sarcasm—hardly said a word. She just sipped her hot
chocolate and stared darkly at the table.

Chapter 9

※※

WITH the radio tuned to a talk station so Rob could practice his Irish brogue, Dr. Dale drove us through low, rusty hills littered with rocks. "This is called the Burren, but it's certainly not barren." We got an earful about the unusual variety of plant life, for the sake of Skid's travel report. Reece hardly said a word. Her excitement about Mei and the search for the sword had washed out to sea.

We got out to stare at rocks. Reece pretended to look for flowers, but I knew better. She wanted distance from the rest of us. I followed her to the stone fence. "You okay?"

"Fine," she said, but her heart wasn't in it.

"Lots of rocks here," I said stupidly.

She straightened up and looked at me with a long, sad, searching look. "The winds and the waves obey him." It wasn't her usual Bible voice; I thought she was going to cry.

We were an hour farther up the coast before I understood what Reece meant, but Rob was sitting between us, so I couldn't bring it up.

It made no sense to me that on the week of Halloween most of the B&Bs were full. In America people don't travel far, except up and down streets for treats. We stopped at houses of every shape and size with big driveways and labeled "B&B." A few had vacant rooms, but not enough for all of us. We had to settle for a place with no green shamrock on the sign out front, meaning it was not recommended by the tourist board. It looked fine to me.

Dr. Dale pulled in. "This will have to do. We can't be searching for lodging after dark." He winked cheerfully at Dr. Eloise. "After that sand spider incident in our tent outside old Babylon, how bad could this be?"

She shuddered. "Shall we not talk about that?!"

We wanted details, but Dr. Eloise frowned forebodingly.

The lady of the house reminded us of Miss Flewharty. She was thin and brittle in a print dress and gray sweater. Her son was just plain weird: a moon-faced kid who slumped and shuffled and stared at the girls.

The lady ushered us into the entry hall. "Yer rooms are upstairs, but could ya wait here? I'm a-hoov'rin' the rug. Won't take but a minute." She dashed up the stairs.

Dr. Eloise leaned over to her husband. "They're unprepared. Not a good sign."

We guys stayed in a cramped, chilly room with bunks and a twin bed. A narrow homemade shelf held an electric teapot and cups. We had a stained sink, a closet made from old paneling, and a tall, drafty window, which looked out to the main street. Rob and I took the bunks. We were unpacking when there was a knock at the door.

"Who is it?" Rob asked in a singsong voice.

A whisper penetrated the door. "It's me, Eloise."

She slipped in clutching a bag, said "Shhh!" and dumped

the bag onto Skid's bed: dish soap, disinfectant spray, a scouring pad. "I can't let you boys sleep in this squalor." She set to work scrubbing out the teapot and cups, thumping dust out of the tea bags, scouring the sink, and beating the pillows. A toxic cloud of feathers and spray chemicals hung in the air as she made us tea and warned us about the basket of snacks on the nightstand. "Individually wrapped, but who knows how long they've been there?"

I asked if I could call my mom.

"Tomorrow, dear. There's a stiff charge for using the phone. She huffed. "No shamrock indeed! And that boy! Acts like a Peeping Tom! I've told the girls to chock a chair against their door. It wouldn't hurt for you to do the same."

She wished us a crisp good-night and slipped out, sticking her head back in to whisper, "We're across the hall. Don't go to the girls' room now. Breakfast tomorrow at 8:00. I'm sorry, boys. This is our last unapproved no-shamrock lodging place or my name's *not* Eloise Stallard!"

Skid pressed a fist into her shoulder. "This is spiritual warfare, Dr. E—the trenches. We're up for it."

The door closed. Rob unplugged the teapot and whispered uneasily, "One problem. Her name's *not* Eloise Stallard."

We talked in whispers, though we were probably the only people in the house except for Irish Flew and her weird son. After a snack of ammonia-flavored tea and old cookies, we jumped under the covers and turned out the light.

We couldn't sleep, so Skid turned on the radio. As part of the Halloween season, a lady was telling a story, her voice lowered to make it sound eerie:

"It was in the 1700s. Jack the blacksmith, a notorious drunkard, had run up a huge debt over the years. No pub would give him a drink. One night a little man at the bar said," (the lady went into a German accent) "'*Mein freund,* I'll give you money for a drink, but I'm the devil, unt I'll need your soul.' Jack took him up on the deal, had his drink, and then scooped up the devil and put him in his pocket. He dropped a cross in his pocket and said, 'Ha, ha! Now ye won't be able to escape.' But the devil escaped and ran up a tree. Jack carved a cross into the tree so the devil couldn't get down, fer he was afraid of the cross, ya see. He begged Jack to let him down. Jack said, 'I'll let ye down, Old Scratch, but ya must promise never ever to claim my soul.' The devil agreed. So Jack the blacksmith went back to his loathsome ways and died an early death. At the pearly gates St. Peter said, 'Jack, ye're a terrible man; ye can't come in,' and sent him to Hell. The devil said, '*Mein freund,* I can't claim your soul. I'm a man of me verd. You must vahnder zee oontervurld for eternity.' Then Jack said, 'Ah, but 'tis so dark out there in the underworld.' So the devil picked up a glowing ember and threw it at Jack, who was eating a turnip like any good Irish chap fresh out of Hell. He cut a hole in the turnip and put the ember inside to light his way through the underworld. So that's the story," the lady told her listeners. "When the Irish immigrated to America, they brought Halloween with them. But instead of hollowing out turnips for Jack lanterns, the Americans recommended pumpkins."

The program went into a round of Irish folk music, and Skid turned it off. "Skidmore," I said in the darkness, "that story's just made up, but this stuff about the devil. What is . . . real?"

"Most of what you hear is not real," he answered. "Red horns and tail and pitchfork, making deals for your soul—most people don't know squat about the truth."

"And you do?" Rob asked.

"I have voodoo in my background."

"Is that where you learned it?" I asked.

"Everyone has an opinion about the devil, Creek. You don't go to backwater slaves or anybody else for answers. You go to the Quella. It doesn't say much about what he looks like—serpent, dragon, angel of light. But it tells a lot about what he does. You can look him up tomorrow. But Satan is real, we're clear on that. Demons are real and Hell is real. Dad says, 'Dabble in it, boy, and get sucked into the abyss.' That's what Dad says."

"But we're *men* now," said Rob boldly. "We're world travelers; we can handle it."

"Nothing to do with manhood, Wingate."

It got quiet for a minute. I asked Skid, "Your parents believe the same as you, right?"

"Yeah."

"I don't think my parents believe in God and Heaven and Hell much. They don't talk about it."

Skid said, "My dad's always asking: 'When does a man of God start his eternal life? When does he cross that line?'"

Rob said, "Your dad's not much help in the answer department, is he? Big on rules, weak on answers."

"Hey, your dad's no prize, Wingate."

I heard Rob turn over and settle in for the night. With the Irish accent he'd been working on, he said, "Don't cha be dissin' me dad, Marcus, or ye'll find yerself a-shiverin' out there on the quay in the blinky of an eyelet."

I told the guys what Dr. Dale had said at the Cliffs of Morte about one of us being targeted by the evil one.

"Who?" Rob asked.

"He didn't know."

It got quiet for a long time. I thought I heard shuffling in the hall. I crept to the door, listened, unlocked it quietly, then flung it open. But no one was there.

I wanted to stay awake sorting through questions like: What is the veil between the worlds, and does it really get thin on Halloween? If Satan wants someone, how does he go about getting him? Could all the magics of the world be hidden in Ireland, even the sword of the Lord? And I wanted to keep an ear on the door, but jet lag got the best of me.

We survived the night at the no-shamrock inn and met for breakfast downstairs. Irish Flew had a huge spread: eggs and sausage, different kinds of bread, and strong dark tea. Eloise didn't eat much, and from the way she looked at her plate, I figured she was leery of food not approved by the tourist board. Dr. Dale had tea and juice but no solid food. They arranged for Skid and Reece to be at their table, partly to give them pointers for their school projects. But my hearing being very acute, I was able to pick up whispery questions about what Rob and Mei believed. Skid said under his breath that Rob hadn't yet done the saved stuff it talks about in the Bible. I couldn't pick up what Reece said about Mei, but Dr. Eliose mentioned God's patience.

At our table Mei filled us in on life in London. "It's very wonderful. I attend Sahara's school to study English and European history. It's very difficult! But I prayed to see you again, and God answered my prayers! Sahara is so nice. They live very differently, so it is a good culture experience."

"What do you mean—different?" I asked.

"Her mother has a husband and a boyfriend. Her father has a girlfriend. They all live together with the children. This doesn't happen in Japan!! They have an herb garden and sell magical mixes and amulets and oils."

She took her cup of tea in both hands and sipped. Shyly she said, "I missed you all so hard that I cried. Tell me what is happening in Magdeline. I want to hear!"

We filled her in on our clubs and sports and how I got

burned rescuing the shield of faith. I showed her my scar, which had healed over. I'd missed having the whole group together and felt a pang. *We only have a week, then it's back to Magdeline, Emma . . . and Miss Abner with her Roman hordes.*

On the way to the north shore, we stopped off to get gas. While the others went into a card shop, I cornered Dr. Dale.

"Hey, um . . . ," I asked, "did you believe what Mei said about all the mysteries and magics being hidden away?"

"No."

"But it bothers you."

"The influence of myths over her spirit concerns me. The problem with pagan religions is this: there is little or no revelation and much fabrication."

"You're talking college level. I'm a high school freshman."

"Of course. Revelation means truths about God revealed by God himself as opposed to fabrication: stories made up from experiences and folk tales."

"But I noticed you quit eating after Mei said that."

All he said was, "We'll discuss it later." I wondered if he was on a vision quest.

We drove along Lough Foille, a huge inlet bay of ocean. We argued about how to pronounce it until we passed Ballykelly Forest where Rob went into a spiel about how every place is named Bally-something.

"*Bally* means 'town,'" said Mei. "I'm learning three Englishes: American, British, and Irish. Too much vocab!"

Now that she'd warmed up to us again, Mei did more talking than Reece. Being an artist, she was interested in all the greens of the Emerald Isle. "It is very beautiful here, but I must brag about Japan. There is no green as beautiful as rice fields in August. Someday you must see them."

We reached the high and rocky north coast, edging along the cliffs above the North Atlantic. The sun was shining, and the ocean was blue. The storm had blown over, and we were in high spirits, except for Reece. Around a curve Dunluce Castle suddenly came into view: a huge, ragged, stone ruin perched on the very edge of the cliff.

I whispered to Reece, "This could be the place!"

No answer.

We parked above the castle in a parking lot surrounded by a wet, sloping, green meadow that smelled like sheep. I held Reece back from the others. "What's up?"

"Nothing." She struggled along, her cane sinking into the soggy ground with every step.

I stuck by her. "C'mon. You mad at me?"

"Of course not. We have a sword to find. Let's get to it."

Dr. Eloise gathered us at the gate. "This place appears to be nothing more than a shell. There is no roof, no windows, or furnishings. We have read that a secret passage goes down to the sea to a cave where sailors often hid. It's unsafe and therefore locked." She glanced knowingly at Dr. Dale. "We'll take a look around and then regroup here in thirty minutes."

The girls went off together. Skid and I walked around the outside fence and peered down into a deep chasm that separated us from the castle. He said, "I bet at high tide it fills with water. That's one serious moat."

We wandered through what used to be a house and chapel but were now only broken walls of sun-washed stone. Rob found us and gave us his version of the info sheet: "It's believed that the two round towers and some of the outer walls were built by MacMerrits, who controlled the north coast in the 1300s, blah blah . . . soft basalt made up of round boulders, inclined to erode . . . Sorley Boy MacDonnell. Ha, funny name . . . In 1636 a new owner built a manor house for big parties. The duchess hated the sound of the sea and with good reason: one night during dinner the whole kitchen and the servants working in it fell into the sea."

We found the drop-off place and looked down a long time. I don't know why it didn't bother me after what had happened the day before. I couldn't get Dr. Dale's warning out of my mind though. Who did Satan want? What if it was Reece?

Rob went on, "The duchess made an inventory of the castle: a harp, rooms of furniture, curtains, and weapons, which were shipped to their new home. But it doesn't say where that is."

Suddenly it struck me that Dowland would have stood here and read this page. "If Dowland was shopping for armor, this would have grabbed his attention."

Skid looked doubtful. "It's a stretch."

Reece wouldn't go near the wall overlooking the sea despite my efforts to cheer her up. "It's a great day. The sun is shining, it's warm, and we're all together again, just like summer. Can you believe we're here in Ireland?"

She looked at me, her lip quivering. "Even the winds obey him, Elijah."

"I know what you meant back there in the Burren. But God wouldn't do that to you. Wind blows over the ocean all the time. You have to put it aside," I told her. "You only have a few days with Mei; then she'll be gone. And we have to find the sword. We have to."

"I know that," she said coldly and walked away, leaving me with a hollow feeling in my chest.

There was nothing in the gift shop but postcards and mugs and key rings. I asked the man behind the counter about the old cache of stuff from the MacMerrit estate.

"Sadly, the furnishings are long gone. After the restoration of 1660, Sir Randal MacMerrit returned from exile and moved to Ballymeade. The clan broke apart during the next two centuries and died out at Leap Castle."

Francine hadn't mentioned Leap Castle. "Where is that?"

"You'll find 'er in the belly of Ireland. At one time the most haunted castle in all of Europe, she was. Gruesome history around the chapel, which housed its own relics and religious articles."

"What about swords and stuff like that? I like swords."

He smiled. "Sorry, lad. Any to survive would be in museums, private collections, or disposed of."

"Thrown away?"

"A warrior and his sword are not easily parted. If a soldier was killed, his sword might be buried with him or ritually drowned in the bogs."

We gathered at the sunny, grassy floor of the manor house ruin and shared what we'd learned. The Stallards were out of breath and smeared with mud.

Rob said, "Where have . . . you were in the secret tunnel?"

Dr. Dale bent over, braced his hands on his knees, and huffed. "We got clearance."

"What was down there?" I asked.

"Picked clean," he said. "We figured it would be."

Rob said, "The sword was with the rest of the armor at the time of the MacMerrits—like in the tapestry at Ballymeade. It must have gotten separated after they lived here."

"Sketchy," Dr. Dale said in an exhausted voice, wiping his brow. "The trail is too sketchy."

Chapter 10

WE stopped at a "chipper" in Ballycastle for fish and fries, or chips as they're called in Ireland. Rob went off on another tangent about how everything in Ireland is named Bally: "Ballymeade, Ballycastle, Ballykelly—it's crazy!"

Dryly Skid said, "Interesting observation . . . Ballyrob."

For the rest of the trip the nickname stuck.

"We have a nice place to stay tonight," said Dr. Eloise as we zipped along a side road, "a retreat house. It's an hour south of Belfast—a historic house on a nature preserve near the bay." She showed us a pamphlet about Murlough House.

"It's pronounced *Murlock,* with a soft *K* sound." Dr. Eloise demonstrated how to push air from the back of our throats. "It's the same as *lough,* which is Gaelic for 'lake.'"

We'd circled around half the country already. Now we were on the east shore, easing onto a narrow gravel lane with seawater lapping the bank on both sides. It looked suspiciously like the entrance to Seven Avon Place. Dr. Dale pointed out places of interest in every direction.

"Aren't we supposed to call Mom sometime?" I asked.

Dr. Eloise said, "Are you worried, dear?"

"That was a dark place we left her at."

"Dark indeed." Dr. Eloise traded glances with Dr. Dale.

"Ireland's gloomy," Reece complained.

At the end of the road, we plunged into a drive surrounded by tall woods with nice landscaping and mowed grass along the sides. "It's a park like Camp Mudj!" Mei said cheerfully.

Reece said anxiously, "I hope our room is better than the first night. That was awful."

By now I was feeling sorry for Mei—with Reece being so down. We leaned forward anxiously in our seats as we approached a clearing and turned the curve. . . .

Mei gasped with joy. Murlough House was a huge, three-story, beige stone manor, but with big windows, a pretty lawn, trimmed shrubs, and a circle drive with a couple of vans parked out front. A big, square entry jutted out from the front.

"We're staying here?" Mei squealed. "It's a mansion!" She hugged Reece, who smiled weakly.

Rob ran up and knocked while Skid and I unloaded luggage. A red-haired lady swung the door open wide. "Hello! You're the group from the States, is that right? I'm Cynthia. I'll show you to your rooms."

The entry hall was wide with nice wood flooring and fancy rugs. There were chairs along the walls and big landscape paintings in golden frames. Our rooms were on the first floor.

"We have dorm rooms upstairs, but there are so few of you that we thought you'd enjoy our homier accommodations."

Mei had a fit about their room: pink flowered bedspreads and curtains, high ceilings, and tall windows that opened out to show flowering bushes and evergreens. Reece said grudgingly, "At least it's warm."

"And cozy!" added Mei. "And beautiful."

The guys' room was the same except the flowered stuff was blue and purple. Cynthia showed us the bathrooms and showers. "Towels are warming in your rooms. We were just having a snack in the kitchen, if you'd like to join us."

A dozen or so college kids were gathered in the big school-type kitchen around plates of cheese and smoked meat, crackers and bread, and cookies. They were friendly and talkative, introducing themselves as being from all over the place: Oklahoma, Germany, Florida, Canada, Taiwan. Dr. Dale told us to circulate and then left suddenly. Dr. Eloise told us that he was very tired. We grabbed plates and dug in. I edged over to Dr. Eloise. "Who are these people?"

"This is a mission house, Elijah, which means that these young people are here to share their faith."

I didn't get what she meant, so I milled around and asked a few of them why they were in Ireland; they all said pretty much the same thing: God had called them here. One explained, "We run after-school programs for children, day camps, prayer journeys for church groups, family retreats—whatever needs to be done."

They seemed like family even though they didn't look or act alike, and they all had different accents. The kitchen was sort of dark and cold, but I got a warm feeling while listening to their stories of how God brought them to

Ireland even when they didn't have the money or their families objected. One guy had been in jail before being a Christian; another had been an atheist. They told how God had turned their lives upside down. I didn't want to go to bed. These guys were nothing like last summer's counselors.

Needing to keep a low profile, we told them about the castles we'd seen and how this was an independent study. They all had advice on what to do in the time we had left in Ireland:

"You have to eat at a chipper. You just have to!"

"Don't eat the black-and-white pudding!"

"If you're in Dublin, don't miss the *Book of Kells.*"

"The Rock of Cashel is my favorite spot."

"Been to the Cliffs of Morte? Awesome, huh?"

Cynthia let me in the office to call Mom. I dialed Ruthie's number. It was almost 11:00, but no one answered. I tried again to be sure I had the right number.

Dr. Eloise came in. "Did you get through?"

"No one's home."

She frowned at her watch but said in a soothing voice, "We'll try again in the morning. She's in God's hands."

We helped clean up the kitchen, the college kids excused themselves, and we hit the showers. Just as we bedded down for the night, music drifted down the hall: a guitar and voices. Skid's voice came out of the dark, "Night devos."

"Huh?" Rob said.

"Devotions—singing, praying, reading the Bible."

I tucked my hands behind my head and listened. Some of the songs I didn't know, but one was the same as from Reece's church. I mentioned it to Skid out of curiosity. "How do these people from all over the world know the same song?"

"Good news travels fast, Creek. You've got a lot to learn about how all this God stuff works."

"How do you know how 'God stuff' works?" Rob snipped.

"I got wise to it at an early age. It's big."

"Bigger than your ego?" Rob jabbed.

"A little bigger than that, Ballyrob." He laughed good-naturedly. "You the man, Wingate."

Maybe it was jet lag, but I slept better than I had in days.

We were on our way out the door into a drizzly new day of sword searching when I remembered Mom. "Wait! I have to make a call!"

Ruthie answered and put Mom right on.

"How's it going?" I asked, relieved to hear her voice.

"It's going," she said weakly.

"Are you okay, Mom?"

"Mm-mmm."

I lowered my voice. "Hey, if there's something wrong on your end, tell me in code, and we'll come and get you. If you're in trouble just say, 'Have you talked to Dad?'"

She half chuckled. "Really, hon. I'm dealing with difficult issues, that's all. Are you having a good time?"

"Yeah. It's awesome. Today we see a five-thousand-year-old tomb; then we're going up on some hill. Tomorrow is Dublin."

Dr. Dale came in and asked to talk to Mom. He told her we needed a few more days and that we'd stay in touch. Then I got back on. "We have to go."

Mom said, "I'll see you soon. Be safe. I love you."

"You too." I hung up and felt dumb for getting spooked.

Once we got on the road, Dr. Eloise turned to me: "How's the research on Caesar coming?"

I scratched my head. "I don't know where to start."

At the next small-town museum, we pulled over. "Pile out!" she barked. "For Elijah's sake!"

They had some pretty cool stuff—though nothing about Roman hordes. But what stopped me in my tracks was a standing stone on display with inscriptions carved in it. I snagged Skid as he sauntered by. "Hey, does that look familiar?"

"Yeah, it's called a rock."

"No, the slashes in the stone."

In three seconds he had it: "The shield."

When we called Dr. Dale over, he said, "Ah yes, standing stones. They're all over the British Isles. It says in the brochure they were used to mark boundaries and calculate solar and lunar measurements."

"The slashes look like the rays on the shield," I said.

He examined the stone more closely. "My word—I believe you have something! Eloise?"

Chapter 10

They went to talk to the lady at the desk, and by the time we were ready to leave, they had the lowdown. "The script is spelled *O-G-H-A-M* and pronounced *Oh-yam*. Prehistoric Ireland had no written language, so this one was devised or adopted to keep general records. She'll mail us a copy of the alphabet."

"Irish language is too complicated for me," I said. "The words don't sound anything like they look. At least Latin looks like what it sounds like."

We stopped at a coffee shop for Dr. Dalc to refill his flask. It was crowded, so I wandered back out to the street and stood under the awning out of the drizzle for some peace and quiet. Dr. Eloise wouldn't have it; she poked her head out the door. "Stay with the group, Elijah. We shouldn't get separated. Are you . . . all right?"

"Dr. Eloise, can I ask you a question?"

"Certainly." She came out and stood beside me.

"Do you think we went into that visitors' center because we were . . . supposed to, so we could find those letters?"

"Yes, I do. But if we had not gone in, he would have found another way to tell us. God is not limited by our choices."

"And one more thing," I changed the subject. "Maybe you noticed that Reece has been in sort of a bad mood?"

"She's been unusually quiet. That near fall at the Cliffs of Morte disturbed us all."

"Well, she wonders if . . . if since God rules the wind and the waves, if maybe he tried to . . ."

Her face went slack. "Oh, dear Heaven!!" She ran back into the coffee shop where Reece and Mei were buying muffins. "Reece, dear heart, if God had wanted you dead, we'd be calling your mother with the sad news of your demise! We'd be planning a memorial service! God does not *try to do* anything! He only *does* things!"

Reece shot me an acid look for telling on her.

Back in the van we got another load of lecture from Eloise. "About the Cliffs of Morte and life in general, children, God may spare us from tragedy or he may not—"

"It's his call," I interrupted.

"Exactly. If God wants to kill us, he can . . . no, that's not what I mean . . . though he could, not that he *would.*"

It was Dr. Dale's turn to interrupt. "What Eloise is trying to say is this: the evil one's best trick is to attack the character of the Almighty. Bad things happen, but God is good. He is good! He will—in the end—make all things plain and wipe every tear from our eyes. We have to trust him."

Chapter 11

WE wound through the drizzly countryside, Skid giving us a running travel commentary for his assignment. "One can't truly see Ireland without a side trip to Newgrange," he said authoritatively. "The road to the ancient—what is it we're seeing, Dr. D?"

"A passage tomb. A tomb accessed by a long tunnel."

"The road to the ancient passage tomb leads the happy traveler through stone-bordered fields of quiet, green pasture. The damp, fresh, pungent fragrance of wafting October air is a refreshing change from the tangy, coastal breezes of Belfast."

"That's very good, Skid!" Mei said.

"Corny as Kansas in August," said Rob, snapping pictures here and there.

We pulled into the parking lot of Newgrange. Rob yelled, "My limerick's done!" He held up his paper proudly and read:

> *There was a young man from Bally*
> *Whose sisters were Ally and Sally.*
> *They all moved away,*
> *And the towns where they stay*
> *Are named Bally and Bally and Bally.*

This prompted another "Skwagack!" out of Dr. Eloise.

At the end of a long, woodsy path sat the visitors' center.

Dr. Dale went to the information desk and came back saying: "The next bus for the tomb site leaves in twenty-five minutes. We have time for a short film that will explain what we are about to see."

"The gift shop looks nice," Mei hinted.

"After the tour we'll get a bite and shop," he said.

Skid had been unusually quiet, and I'd caught him in deep-thought mode a couple of times. When we got seated in the theater and everyone else was talking, I asked, "What do you think of the trip so far?"

"Pretty cool. Pretty cool."

"And?"

"And what?"

"Something you're not saying."

"Don't know how to put it," he shrugged, stretched his legs out, and crossed his arms. "I've traveled a lot, Creek. Been all over. Seen sights, met missionaries, been to churches—I didn't get it. After talking to those college guys, I'm startin' to get what's happening."

The room got dark, and the movie started. Pictures of outer space dissolved into the sun and then closed in on the spinning earth. The narrator explained that all life depends on light, and the ancients feared the dying of the sun every winter when the days shortened. According to him, they worshiped the sun, prayed to it, and built monuments to it all over the world: Stonehenge, the pyramids of Mesoamerica and Egypt.

The movie showed the tomb at Newgrange and all its unsolved mysteries. Who built it? How'd they haul all those rocks—some weighing twenty thousand pounds—dozens of miles to make massive tombs? Why? What did the mysterious carved symbols mean? It struck me that prehistoric civilizations used technology we still haven't figured out.

Sitting there in the dark, I had the urge to ask El-Telan-Yah: *What are you trying to tell me by bringing me here? Is the sword here in the tomb? Am I supposed to be getting something else?*

When the movie ended, Rob leaned over to Skid, "That movie was like your dad: lots of questions, no answers."

Skid slid a threatening eye toward Rob. "We're heading toward a tomb now, Ballyrob, *a tomb.* Watch your step."

"I'm soooo scared!"

Rob and I got a kick out of Skid's big, hairy threats.

Dr. Dale overheard Skid's threat and suggested an immediate opportunity for us children to get some exercise.

Dr. Eloise said, "Let's start by making our way to the bus. It's a five-minute walk."

We walked across a narrow bridge and stopped to watch the swirling, muddy waters of the River Boyne rush under us. The Stallards talked history and kept an eye on Skid and me. As we waited for the bus, Reece came over, and I braced myself to get snipped at for ratting on her to Dr. Eloise.

She whispered, "What *did* you think of Sahara?"

"We only saw her for a few minutes. She's okay, and

I like the accent. But when she talked about rituals and goddesses, I got a strange feeling."

Reece went on. "The reason I asked is—" she glanced over at Mei to be sure she was still out of earshot, "Sahara and her mom are teaching Mei witchcraft. Mei told me last night. Mei thinks that our beliefs are like that. You make up what you want to believe. Should I say something to the Stallards?"

"I don't know. They're not real subtle."

Reece huffed in agreement.

"Hey, by the way, I didn't mean to get you in trouble, but you were . . ."

"I know. I'm trying, okay? I don't know what got into me, doubting God like that. Something just came over me."

"Dr. Dale said one of us may be targeted by the evil one." I was hinting that maybe he had tried to take out Reece or me. But when my heel had tipped back and hit rock where there was no rock before, what was that all about?

"It's probably you he's after," she said matter-of-factly. "Satan hates it when anyone gives his life to God. Salvation is often followed by a spiritual attack."

A chill went through me. "No one told me that."

"Would you have backed out?" she asked.

"No," I said halfheartedly. We watched the swirling waters rush under us. I said to Reece, "I think it's Mei he's after. We don't have much time with her. Do your stuff."

"What stuff?" she smiled curiously.

"Be yourself."

A bus came to pick us up. I sat by Reece in the front seat; Skid pulled Mei down to the seat behind us. I turned to him. "You said you're starting to 'get it.' What did you mean?"

"Oh yeah. People from everywhere going everywhere to spread the word. It's happening already—millions of kids going around the world every year, building houses and churches, teaching little street kids, giving out food and clothes. The college students at Murlough House? That's us in the future, but our mission will be different." He squeezed Mei's neck. "You too, Aizawa. We're the new wave."

I didn't know what he meant by mission and new wave, but it filled me with a strange kind of hope. If you had told me a year ago that I'd be in Ireland on a quest for a mysterious sword with my four best friends, I'd have said you were loons.

In a few minutes, we were standing outside an enormous, grassy mound held in place by a twelve-foot-high wall of white stones. Around the bottom of the mound was a band of rocks as big as refrigerators. The guide, a friendly chubby guy in his twenties, did his spiel about the mysteries of Newgrange. As he led us into the tomb, he warned us tall guys about cracking our heads on the ceiling. The narrow passage was about sixty feet long; huge standing stones made the walls. At the end were three chambers with strange carvings covering the walls: leaves, flowers, diamonds, ovals with lines, and tri-swirls.

Nearly thirty of us crowded into the center where the three small chambers met. We listened to how skeletons and pottery had been found in the chambers. Then the guide got to the main point. "On the shortest day of the year—the dark day—the sun rises directly into the stone window above the passage and lights up the chamber. Today is not the winter solstice, so we'll have to demonstrate the amazing effect using artificial light."

He turned out the lights. For a second it was pitch-dark; then a weak beam moved down the passage. When it got to us, it lit the entire room. "When the real sun comes shining in, it's bright and golden—amazing," he said. "Anyone can sign up for the winter solstice tour. But there's a ten-year waiting list and no guarantee it won't be cloudy."

When the other tourists filed out, we stayed behind. The Stallards wanted to ask the guide a few questions. That's when he turned off his spiel and got real with us. "I've stood here when the light comes. A lot of people don't put much stock in spiritual things, but when I'm standing here and the light comes . . . you feel something, as if someone is here."

"The sun goddess?" Mei asked, intrigued.

"Some think so," he said politely. "I believe differently."

"I know what you mean," I said. "When I'm alone in my

woods, he comes. But not just when it's sunny. He comes day or night, cloudy or clear. Anytime."

The guide grinned. "That's what I'm talking about."

I turned to Mei and pointed upward. "The creator."

Mei nodded thoughtfully. *"Souzousha."*

Dr. Eloise glowed. "Deuteronomy 4:19 says, 'When you look up to the sky and see the sun, the moon and the stars—all the heavenly array—do not be enticed into bowing down to them and worshiping things the LORD your God has apportioned to all the nations under heaven.'" She went into another verse.

Leaving Dr. Eloise in her own little, happy cloud, Dr. Dale said to the guide, "We don't want to keep you longer or miss our bus, but I'm intrigued by what motivated the ancients to build these structures. They must have lived in huts or tents. Yet to honor their dead, they created this enormous mound. It seems that from the very beginning, the ancients knew there was eternal life. Enoch, the seventh from Adam, didn't die, so they knew it was possible to live forever."

"Getting to the next life was important to these people," the guide answered. "Something else might interest you folks. See how this grave is a long passageway with three chambers, one to the left, one to the right, and one ahead? Well, here's how it would look from the air if you had x-ray vision." He knelt down and drew in the dirt. "Here's the mound of earth, a large circle, and here's the passage tomb inside."

Reece gasped. "A cross-shaped passage to eternal life?"

Dr. Dale said in amazement, "Three thousand years before Jesus was crucified!"

The guide nodded mysteriously and looked at me. "Coincidence?"

When we got out of the tomb, I turned back to the guide. "Hey, when people first discovered this tomb, all they found was bones and pottery?"

"That's about it."

"No . . . armor?"

He shook his head. "Bowls . . . a few Roman coins."

"Roman? Did the Roman hordes attack here?" I added, "I have a research paper to write."

"Some say Caesar invaded and occupied. Some say he didn't."

"Well, if he didn't, why not?"

He shrugged. "I dunno. Too far to haul all that battle gear? Not enough plunder? Caesar didn't like the druids and their ceremonies."

"Thanks." I shook his hand. "I don't guess you could you say that in Latin and stretch it out to two pages?"

On our way back down the hill, Dr. Eloise said, "One more thing we have to clear up, children. Many people marvel at the intelligence and ingenuity of the ancients. Where did this technology beyond our own come from? Were aliens involved, some ask? I believe those inquiring minds are working under a false assumption: that mankind is evolving. According to the second law of thermodynamics, we are *de*volving, running down. Let's mentally travel back through time several millennia to people who lived for hundreds of years and built monuments like these. What do you have?"

Rob said, "Super-intellects?"

"Super-strong super-intellects?" I suggested.

"Super-cool ancients!" Skid threw his hands out.

"That's precisely my theory." She looked back sadly at the mound on top of the hill overlooking the River Boyne. "Superior intellect is not always wise. Death cults as practiced by the ancient Egyptians and Sumerians—all those who built great tombs filled with possessions for the next world—they didn't understand that you can't take it with you."

We stopped for lunch at a pub and got a table by a fireplace—to take the chill out of our bones, as Dr. Eloise said. Dr. Dale ordered soup. The rest of us got big sandwiches. Halfway through the meal, Dr. Eloise said, "Children, we are going to skip our trip to the Hill of Slane this afternoon. Dr. Dale needs to rest. So I'll be driving from here on out."

We all shot him worried looks.

"I'm fine, I'm fine," he said. But his usual spark and energy were gone. His walk was slower, and his back was a little bent. Dr. Dale was acting his age, which worried me.

"Devolving?" Rob joked.

"A little," he said with a half smile.

Reece said, "Can we do anything to help? We'll be quieter. We can do the searching and asking questions."

He patted her hand. "Don't change a thing."

"I can read maps," Rob offered. "I'll be the navigator."

"Thank you," said Dr. Dale. "A half day of rest when we arrived would have braced me for the roundabouts and the spiritual uncertainties. A bit of a strain, that's all."

He was tired, but some big worry was going on in that high-IQ brain of his. Did he worry that the sword was one of the magics hidden for all time? The thought kept creeping into my mind. And what good is armor if you have no sword to defend yourself? None, if you ask me.

We stopped at a couple of antique shops—with no luck—before heading back to Murlough House. Dr. Eloise turned over all their pamphlets and gave us the rest of the day to work on our projects. "Read up on Patrick of Ireland, Elijah. You might find helpful material, a new slant to your topic." She helped Dr. Dale to his room.

Chilling in my blue and purple flowered room, I cranked out a limerick about how hard Irish is:

> *Skid said, "Lough rhymes with tough."*
> *Reece said, "Lough rhymes with through."*
> *Then I said, "Somehow*
> *Lough must rhyme with bough."*
> *But it's Irish. So lough rhymes with rock!*

I thought it was cool until I tried to read it out loud and

sounded ridiculous. So I gave up, took a nap, and tried not to worry about Dr. Dale.

The college kids came bounding in that afternoon. They were about to ask if we'd like to help fix dinner that night when Dr. Eloise burst from her room. "We forgot! It's *Samhain!* Tonight! To the Hill of Slane!!"

Chapter 12

LOOKING weaker than ever, Dr. Dale was still behind the wheel, his wife barking road numbers as we whipped through the roundabouts for the next two hours. We zoomed past a small sign: "Hill of Slane." He slammed on the brakes, turned back, shot up a narrow street, and pulled up to a metal gate. Through the gate and nearly at the crest of the hill lay a cemetery and the remains of a church, the stones black with mold and age. "Patrick's hill of destiny," Dr. Eloise beamed at me.

Except for a couple of crumbling church towers and Celtic crosses poking up everywhere, it could have been Old Pilgrim's graveyard.

From the Hill of Slane, we could see in all directions: rolling farms green as summer but soft and mellow under the butter-colored sky. Not a sound could be heard. Everyone was awestruck. "It's so beautiful!" Reece said reverently. "So awesome . . . to be here . . . together."

"Hi, Mom," I said under my breath toward the southwest. "Hi, Grandma."

Rob turned to me, looking puzzled. "Yeah, we could have a new grandma in a few days? That is too strange."

Standing as still as the tombstones around us, we watched the sun disappear and the sky turn to amber. My eyes left the sunset to glance at Reece standing beside me. Her face was pure gold. Behind her, circled crosses were silhouetted against the yellow sky with hazy, dreamy hills beyond. It seemed to me that I'd slipped into another world.

Reece's eyes, fixed on the sun's disappearing, welled up with tears. Her sniffles turned to sobs. No one had to tell me what she was thinking—she was sorry she'd been so angry at God. I put my arm around her. She folded herself into me and cried some more.

"Look southward," came Dr. Dale's voice from behind me. "See that clump of trees? That's the Hill of Tara. Sixteen centuries ago the high kings of Tara ruled from that hill. Once a year the king would order all fires extinguished. Then on the eve of his druid festival, the priest would light a fire. No one dared defy the custom. But in the year 433, young Patrick climbed this hill and lit a fire to signal the coming of the true light to Ireland. He set his face against the traditions of a whole country—a dangerous thing for one so young and alone."

"What happened to him?" Reece pulled away and wiped her eyes.

Mei was all ears.

Dr. Eloise took up the story. "He was immediately summoned to the king's court, as the story goes. But the king was greatly impressed with Patrick's gospel message and allowed the young missionary to live. It is said that the druids warned the king . . ." Dr. Eloise lowered her voice,

"'If you let that fire burn, O high king, it will never be put out.'" She looked across the land with a satisfied smile. "And so it is. The fire of truth still burns."

Dr. Dale looked at me. "And so it must continue until the end. The fire must not go out." He turned and walked away.

Rob discovered a crumbling spiral stair to one of the small towers. "Come on, guys! It looks dangerous, but it's not. Reece, you can make it."

In a minute all four of them were up there clowning around. Skid peeked out a window from the top, enjoying his new love of heights. "Hey, Creek, come on up!"

"Maybe later." I skimmed the darkening land. *Here one young guy took a stand and changed the world.* One guy. House lights sparked to life one by one . . . and another light high on a hill . . . like the fires of Council Cliffs.

I called Dr. Dale over. "What's that?"

He sighed. "That is the Hill of Ward."

"Where Sahara is?"

"Yes. A pagan fire is lit tonight; worshipers invite unknown entities to come through the veil. Here and around the world . . . on this night and every night. Fires lit to gods who are inventions of the mind, or worse: demons in disguise."

Spread out before me was a black world, a crimson sky, and a decision. Reece had been right when she'd said, "You won't be living the regular life: go to church on Sunday, put a buck in the offering plate, and light a candle at Christmas."

Chapter 12

Watching that fire on the Hill of Ward set a fire in me. Those people were bowing to nothing and calling it something, worshiping evil, convincing Mei that it was all well and good. I stood where Patrick stood, watching what he'd seen sixteen centuries before. I felt what he felt. I watched the fire grow.

"Do you have a match?" I asked Dr. Dale.

I dragged fallen limbs from the trees above the old church, broke them over my knee, and stacked them in a teepee shape on the paved path. All I had for tinder were some damp twigs and leaves. *It'll never catch.* There was trash in the van, but it wouldn't be enough. *Creek, what resources do you have?* Down beyond the gate were a few houses. *Yeah, sure, a foreign teenage guy knocks at your door on Halloween night and asks to borrow stuff to build a fire. That'd go over big.*

Then I remembered how the Mad River Boys did it. I went to Dr. Dale. "I need to siphon some gas out of the van."

Dr. Eloise wrung her hands while Dr. Dale helped me rig up a siphoning hose. I got drinking straws from our fast-food trash bag and stuck them together with surgical tape from the first-aid kit. I used his coffee flask to catch the gas. The other four convinced Dr. Eloise that I knew what I was doing and had years of training, that I wasn't a pyro.

In the end it wasn't much of a fire—even with a couple of flasks of gasoline thrown on for good measure—but it was a fire. I kept it going while the Stallards explained to Mei the big difference between Sahara's fire and my fire.

Stars popped out all over the universe. If you know one thing about astronomy, you understand that some old god of the sun couldn't hold a candle to the creator of a whole doggone universe. The Stallards didn't have to drive the point home to any of us. God did it himself with a cosmic show of force: the Milky Way, billions of suns. He even threw in a meteor shower for good measure.

Dr. Dale got a flashlight and beamed it on his open Bible. "This is a passage from the *Warrior*." His voice was thick and powerful as he read: "'Why do the nations conspire and the peoples plot in vain? The kings of the earth take their stand and the rulers gather together against the LORD and against his Anointed One. . . . The One enthroned in heaven laughs; the Lord scoffs at them. . . . O LORD, how many are my foes! How many rise up against me! Many are saying of me, 'God will not deliver him.' But you are a shield around me, O LORD; you bestow glory on me and lift up my head. To the LORD I cry aloud, and he answers me from his holy hill!"

Silence fell around my crackling fire. Skid looked at me, his green eyes wide and watery in the semi-dark, his voice low and awed. "This is what I meant, man. We're the new wave."

I understood in my head about good waging war on evil. God and Satan. In some way, though, I was still out of the loop. But all that was about to change.

On the way back, Dr. Dale told the others about Patrick

and Brendan and Columba, the *peregrini* who wandered the world—never sure where they were going, or if they'd return.

The college kids had saved leftovers for us, and we stood around in the big kitchen, chowing down until the wee hours. I did a lot of listening that night.

Later when they were having devos, I crept down the hall toward their meeting room. I eased myself to the cold floor, leaned against the wall, and listened. None of them were great singers, but together it was the nicest sound. Over and over I pictured myself on the Hill of Slane. I watched the sunset; I kept holding onto Reece; I gathered wood. I felt the flames shooting heavenward with Skid's words ringing in my mind: *we're the new wave.* We'd made no headway finding the sword that day, but I wouldn't have traded my moment on the Hill of Slane for a million bucks.

It was the morning of the fourth day. We'd had four hours of sleep, but the Stallards were up and packed by 8:00. Dr. Dale was gray with exhaustion, but his eyes were clear and intense. There was a mysterious calm around him, like he knew something we didn't. We thanked Cynthia for our breakfast of eggs and thick Irish bread with tea, and loaded the van.

Dr. Eloise jumped behind the wheel. "Driving in Dublin will be suicide!"

"Greaaaat," Skid said smoothly.

Rob took navigator position, and Dr. Dale sat in the

back. We pulled onto the main highway and Rob barked, "A25 to Newry where we catch A1 to M1 and all the way to Dublin."

Skid quipped, "Man the lifeboats, my people," then went off ad-libbing another travelogue. "After a grand breakfast of sumptuous eggs and hearty tea, we depart for Dublin. Pungent air awakens the lungs, and quaint villages invite the eager traveler."

Ballyrob threatened to hurl up his sumptuous eggs and hearty tea if Skid didn't shut up.

"To spare our lives and our sanity," Dr. Eloise threw her voice in our direction as she whipped us around the roundabout and shot off onto A25, "we'll park on the outskirts and take a lovely little train into the heart of the city. We'll have a look at the *Cathach,* the oldest surviving manuscript in Ireland, written down by Columba. The *Warrior,* Dale, the *Warrior!*"

We made it to Sandyford station where we boarded a silver commuter train. We zipped through the outskirts and got off at St. Stephen's Green, a nice, woodsy park with a lake and stream right downtown. Skid started in again. "Around the green, Dublin's downtown traffic bustles along through the quaint but modern city of stone and brick, trimmed in dark, rich colors. No, my friends, Dublin isn't a high-rise metropolis like Chicago, but the friendly faces—"

Reece broke in with a singsong, "I'm in Dublin with Me-i, I'm in Dublin with Me-i."

They hugged and giggled. I breathed a sigh of relief. The evil one had let go of his gloomy grip on Reece.

"Another museum?" Skid muttered as we headed into a huge, gray stone building.

"Now, now. This is for our artist, " said Dr. Eloise, smiling at Mei. "But I believe we'll all appreciate the art of manuscript decoration. The *Book of Kells* is perhaps the world's most exquisite book. A quick look, then we must track down the *Warrior*."

The museum had a film showing how people made books from scratch twelve hundred years ago: pens from quills, pages from animal skins, paint from plants and minerals, ink from charcoal. Back then making one lousy book was two tons of work. They made it a whole lot fancier than they needed to because it was the Bible.

After the hard driving, we were glad to be hanging out, strolling along cobblestone streets, checking out the Irish city folks. I was starting to feel a little guilty that we weren't chasing down the sword, when I noticed a sign on a window: "The Cathach—Coffees Teas Books."

"Hey, let's go there. Maybe they have books about the *Warrior*!"

It was a tiny café with a few tables connected to a bookstore—even smaller—with floor-to-ceiling shelves and a ladder on wheels. A circular iron staircase led down to a basement. The owner was standing in his little office in the back. He stepped out. "May I help you?"

"We're looking for books on the—" I tried to say it right, "*Caa'thuck*!"

"Gesundheit!" said Rob.

The owner looked down his rimless glasses at me. "That sort would be downstairs. Liam will aid you." He stepped back into his doorway like a guardian soldier.

I peered down the stairs and saw a handful of shoppers jammed in the boxy little room. "It looks crowded down there. I'll go."

Rob said, "We'll check out the menu. I'm starved already."

A polite-looking guy not much older than I, with dark hair and green eyes, was restocking shelves.

"Do you have any books on the *Cathach*?" I asked.

He looked blank. "I don't know."

"Since your store is called that name, I thought—"

"We deal in history, folklore . . . divination."

"It's part of the Bible, the Psalms."

"I doubt we have anything on it," he said flatly.

"Would you mind looking?" I pressed. As he ran a finger along the titles, I pulled out a book and started idly flipping through it. "Yeah, some experts told me the *Cathach* was used as a good-luck charm for battles. But we're interested in it for *spiritual* warfare. Fighting evil," I said proudly.

I flipped through another book. I became aware that he'd stopped moving. I lifted my eyes from the page. Liam's hand lay quiet on the wall of books, and he stared at the books.

His head rotated mechanically in my direction. His dark eyes drilled into me. His lip curled in disgust, and this total stranger seethed at me with a kind of hate I'd never seen: black, pure hate. From his mouth came a deep rattle of a voice: "You'll never find it."

A quiet roar filled my head—blood rushed through my brain. I seemed to go numb. But a corner of my mind stayed perfectly clear. I knew without looking that there were only two of us in the basement. The other customers had left. But there was a third. Two bodies, three beings. It wasn't Liam talking. It was something else. Liam wasn't referring to the *Cathach*. He was talking about the sword.

Still sneering, his eyes slid back to the wall of books as if nothing had happened. I backed away without a word and went up the steps in a daze.

"Any luck?" Reece met me at the top. One look at my face and she said, "What happened?!"

"Nothing," I muttered. "They didn't . . . uh . . . don't . . . have anything."

Her eyebrows shot up excitedly, a simple, sudden gesture that nearly made me jump out of my skin. "Well, don't go to pieces, Elijah! We'll see the real thing this afternoon. This is a side trip; our real quest is the sword."

"Yeah." I glanced around to see if we'd been overheard.

Skid came over. "You look shook. I can't believe the prices either; I could buy a new skateboard for one book the size of a piece of toast! Let's go."

"Yeah," I murmured weakly, "let's go."

I couldn't think. The hate from those eyes and that growling voice hung on me like a stench. I wanted to wash it off. I wanted to be baptized again.

"Cheer up, Creek," Skid insisted. "Isn't it weird that a store by the name of a book has no copies of the book, and even no books about it? Weird."

"Yeah."

"I know you're hungry, children," said Dr. Eloise, "but we need to try to view the *Cathach* if we can. It shouldn't take long. Elijah, aren't you feeling well?"

"I'm okay," I said.

We got directions to the Grafton Institute from someone on the street. Everyone was so friendly; the Stallards said getting around Ireland was easier than other places they'd been where few speak English or where Americans are generally disliked. "Most everyone here has a distant relative in the States," said Dr. Eloise. "We Americans love Ireland's people. What a nice arrangement between countries!"

I was going through the motions, my mind still on what happened in the basement of the bookstore. *It was a demon. A demon.* My mind in a fog, I tagged along behind the others down a tree-lined street to what looked like a town house. A fancy sign out front read: "Grafton Institute."

Dr. Dale paused, his hand at the door knocker. "Eloise, we are doing the right thing, aren't we?"

"I think we have no choice," she answered. "We have one

more lead, Leap Castle, which seems to be long abandoned and under renovation. After that it's a dead end."

He looked at us. "Let us be cautious not to reveal any secrets about the sword. Let Eloise and me do the talking."

Dr. Eloise seemed torn. "They're antiquities people. What if they've heard of . . . the armor?"

"It would certainly complicate things," he answered, gripping the door knocker. "We've had this on our hearts for years—we've searched and made inquiries. We would have crossed paths with these people before, if they knew anything."

"Yes, of course. They're not a part of the network. We've been thorough and careful, haven't we?"

"Very."

He knocked. In a minute a heavy, old gentleman in a black suit came to the door. "We're closed today."

"I'm Dr. Dale and this is my wife Eloise. These are our students. I spoke with someone on the phone about an important matter, about the *Cathach*."

Skid and I swapped glances. He'd made it sound like Dale was his last name. He didn't want to be traced.

"I didn't take a call. We'll be open fifth November." He started to close the door.

"Wait!" Dr. Dale pulled out the page enclosed in the plastic sleeve. "You must see what we found!"

The door opened again. The man's eyes fell on the page. He did a double take. Dr. Eloise put her hand on the door. "We believe it's authentic."

Dr. Dale put the page back in his briefcase. Reluctantly the man let us in. "Cravens is the name." He took us to his office, and Dr. Dale laid his briefcase on the big desk.

Cravens started asking questions. "Where did you get this page, if you don't mind my asking?"

Dr. Eloise said, "We'd like to see the *Cathach* first, please."

"Certainly. Now what organization did you say you're with?" he asked cleverly.

They dodged instead of answering. Cravens wanted answers first. They wanted to see the book. Finally he caved and led us to a back room to a stack of flaky old pages like the *Book of Kells,* locked under glass with special lights. Cravens unlocked the case, gently pulled out the book, and laid it on the glass. He asked to see the page again. As Dr. Dale placed it on the glass, Cravens's eyes were glazed with excitement, his expression deadpan. "Are there more pages?"

"Not from this source."

"What source would that be?"

Dr. Eloise glanced at her husband, pulled the gold opera glasses out of her bag, and viewed the *Cathach* from where she stood. "We found the page in a spoiled old thing, a piece of armor. It's been fiddled with, redone, no story, no papers on it. The page was used as stuffing in the back of a shield, of all things! We tracked the language to Irish Gaelic and . . . voilà!" She paused. "We love antiques—European things especially. We'd be happy to turn the page over to . . ."

I gasped.

Up to this time Cravens had hardly noticed us, being intent on the lost page.

I cleared my throat as if there was dust in the room, which was dumb because dust is not allowed in fancy archive rooms. Dr. Eloise, cool as a cucumber, turned to me smiling. "Catching a cold?" But her eyes shot me a cautious look. *Don't blow my cover.*

"What we'd really like in exchange—" Dr. Dale started.

Cravens broke in. "This a private institute, small. We're not heavily endowed."

"No, no, I'm not talking money. We were curious about the origin of the shield from which we extracted this page. We'd love to have an entire set from the period, a helmet and sword and so on, for our entryway. Even just the shield and a sword would look marvelous over our mantle. So if you had any information in your extensive archives about a shield . . . or a sword connected with the *Cathach*—"

Ever so slowly Cravens began to change. His big jowls quivered for a second. He went rigid. I felt like a witness to a drug deal. Nothing was said for a very long moment. The doctors and the archivist locked onto each others' faces, looking for signals. Cravens glanced at us kids suspiciously.

"You're from America," he said at last, "and you came all this way for a mantle decoration?"

"This is primarily an educational tour." Dr. Eloise smiled at us. "Antiquing is merely a diversion."

Cravens didn't buy it for a minute.

Something was up. Dr. Eloise glanced at Dr. Dale and blinked in code.

Cravens bent over the page again. "It's authentic. One of the missing pages from the *Cathach*. We had no idea any of them still existed." He strolled around the table, circling us. Our eyes followed him; we didn't move. He said in an oozing voice, "Yes, yes, the world has its unsolved mysteries, doesn't it? The far-fetched, the mythical, on which no respectable man of science would waste his time or risk his career. Myths," he said in my ear as he circled. "UFO landings," he said to Skid, and around the circle, "Noah's ark . . . the lost city of Atlantis . . . the lost pages of the *Cathach* . . ." He moved around to Dr. Dale and hissed, "The armor of God . . ."

The Stallards tried hard not to wilt.

He completed the circle and stood facing us in the dim archival light.

Dr. Dale said matter-of-factly, "Interesting myths aside, we're simply looking for a sword of a period that might match the shield we have."

"You have the other pieces?"

"Of what?"

A smile slithered crossed Cravens's shadowy face. "I believe they'll find Atlantis one day and the Loch Ness Monster. I believe it."

"Me too!" blurted Rob. "Nessie's probably a plesiosaur—"

I elbowed him hard.

The hefty man drew his hands behind him and bent over the lost page. "And I believe that wandering the world is a relic that is not a relic, a thing that spans all time, a thing that comes together only with great power, then disappears like a wanderer in the bogs, only to reappear again—when it's . . . ," he locked eyes with Dr. Dale, "needed."

"Quite an interesting theory you have, Mr. Cravens," Dr. Dale said with finality. "We've taken enough of your time."

Cravens went on greedily, "A treasure of immeasurable wealth. No man can purchase it, for it cannot be appraised."

Smugly, Dr. Eloise spoke into the handle of her opera glasses, "Thank you so much, Mr. Cravens of Grafton Institute. If we happen upon anyone in the scientific community, we'll be sure to let them know of your interest in UFOs and Nessie and those other—" she chuckled lightly, *"legitimate fields of scientific study you mentioned.* I'm sure your colleagues would be delighted to know that." She closed the glasses with a loud click and dropped them into her purse.

Skid and I swapped looks. *She has a tape recorder in those glasses?!*

Dr. Dale picked up the page and slid it into his briefcase. "If we ever decide to sell, we'll give you a call."

Cravens followed us to the door. "And if I find a certain sword, where might I contact you?"

"Good day," said Dr. Dale.

Chapter 13

WE wound through side streets of Dublin, the Stallards glancing back every now and then to see if we were followed. We slipped into a pizza place and got an upstairs table in a back corner. They ordered smoked salmon with crème fraiche. I got good old American pepperoni. When the waitress left, Dr. Eloise said sarcastically, "That went well! He knew, Dale, he knew! What were the chances?"

"Perhaps greater than we previously thought," said Dr. Dale nervously.

They were pretty upset. None of us knew what to do. But Reece popped up with, "We still have Leap Castle. Have faith. God wouldn't let us come all this way for nothing."

The afternoon got balmy with good smells of coffee and food. Music of every kind drifted on the air. Dr. Eloise said, "Let's cheer ourselves with the street entertainers."

Some little kid stood on a corner and sang at the top of his lungs; I dropped a coin into his basket. There was a fire-juggling act on one corner and a flute player on the next. A crowd gathered around a folk rock group of three guys with guitars and a portable sound system. They had shaggy hair and were in jeans and black leather jackets. We edged into the crowd to listen. The words of their song were about life not being what you think, that even love is a broken alleluia.

It was sad and beautiful. Reece had tears in her eyes.

This quest wasn't what I thought. *What's going on? Why's this strange stuff happening: Mei living with a witch, Reece and me almost dying, Dr. Dale giving up food and acting mysterious? And some entity telling me I'll never find the sword.*

On down the street, another crowd had gathered at a big intersection to hear a man yelling. I thought it was a politician trying to get himself elected. Dr. Eloise warned, "Stay together now. It could be a militant faction."

A man in his thirties held the mike. His face was square and serious, his eyes sad and piercing. People stood behind him with posters that said "YOUR SIN WILL FIND YOU OUT" and "REPENT AND BELIEVE THE GOSPEL." The preacher paced and yelled above the street noise, "I am not asking you to join a church or to follow some list of rules. I am begging you to give your life to Jesus! The Day of the Lord is coming!"

Some people walked past smirking. Others looked embarrassed for the guy. One woman stood there crying until she was handed a pamphlet. The preacher looked directly at me. "He may be coming soon. Give him your heart!"

"I did!" I said back. "I already did!"

Everyone on that street stopped and stared at me. The preacher himself seemed shocked, but he shouted, "Amen!"

Humiliated, I whirled around and disappeared into the crowd. Reece and Rob called my name, but I kept on walking.

What's going on? God? Why's everyone talking to me? I'm in a foreign country. No one even knows my name, and they're talking directly to me!!

I stopped at another corner where a woman in old-fashioned clothes sat playing a little harp in front of a church door. I leaned against the wall a few feet from her, tossed a coin into her basket and looked around me, wondering how I ended up circling a country looking for a sword that the whole world had lost track of.

After a while I doubled back to find the others. I found one of those pamphlets in the gutter and picked it up. It said: "Eternity . . . where will YOU be?" and the address of the gospel meeting on St. Stephen's Green.

No one in our group mentioned my yelling out, but they gave me odd looks. A drizzle settled in. We went to a pub for hot chocolate. I sat at the end of the table next to Dr. Dale. When the others got engrossed in their souvenirs, I pulled out the pamphlet and showed it to him. "I want to go to this."

He studied it. "This is downtown. We were going to take the train back to the station and the van to Murlough House."

"I know, but I have to go to this. I don't know why."

Everyone debated who should go and why until it was a big mess. Finally I said, "I'm going by myself, and that's it!"

Dr. Dale sighed. He was tired and disappointed in the dead ends. He asked, "Can you get the train back?"

"Sure," I said uncertainly.

"You can catch a cab from the station." He pulled out his wallet and gave me some bills. "If this is something you have to do, here's money for your dinner, train and cab fare."

After a long discussion and more worried looks from the others, we parted ways. I watched the train pull out toward Sandyford. The sun was behind the buildings already. Streetlights flickered on, and the crowds just got bigger. *Don't people go home here? They roll up the streets of Magdeline at dinnertime.* I kept my bearings toward St. Stephen's Green and wandered, engulfed in pure loneliness and confusion. *You'll never find it.* That voice—I couldn't get it out of my mind!

Just before 8:00, I went inside a red brick building and sprinted up the steps to the second floor. A plain-looking man with a red face welcomed me. I recognized him as one of the people holding a doomsday poster.

"Good evenin' and welcome, lad."

"Thanks."

"What's yer name?" he asked.

"Uh . . . Telanoo. George Telanoo."

I felt terrible going to church incognito, but after the meeting with Cravens, I couldn't be too careful. It was the first time I began to understand why the Stallards had changed their names.

"Nice to meet ya, George. Warn't you the lad who—?"

"That was me. I'm . . . uh, saved, so . . ." I shook my head, indicating that I didn't need to be baptized or anything.

"That's grand. So yer comin' to hear the man again?" He nodded approvingly. "He puts the fear of God in ye sideways, don't he?"

"Um, yeah. Fear of God . . . sideways . . . yeah."

It wasn't a usual church but a meeting room—bare except for chairs lined up and a small pulpit. At the back was a snack table of cookies and tea. Off the room was a hallway where moms were taking their little kids.

I picked up a program and took a seat at the back. A lady with a guitar got up and started playing. People joined in with hands raised and eyes closed—sort of like Skid's pentecoastal church meeting but not as rowdy. I didn't know the words, and I'd have felt fake doing the hand raising and eye-closing thing. It was a song about the end of time—darkness and famine and sword. *Sword?? Is this why I'm here? Does someone here know about the sword?* I flipped open the program to see what the song title was. Halfway down the page were the words: "The Days of Elijah."

I tried not to freak.

The street preacher's sermon was interesting partly because of his cool Irish accent. But mostly because he preached about the Elijah in the Bible, how he went up against Baal-Zebub, the lord of the flies, the prince of demons, all by himself. And how he called fire down from Heaven. I hung on every word. Other people liked the sermon too, and went forward to be prayed over or to give their lives to God. Afterwards the preacher and the red-faced man talked a minute. They looked over at me. The preacher came over smiling. "Nice to have you at our service. You from around here?"

"The States."

"I see. First time to Ireland?"

"Yessir."

"You're the one who spoke up today, sayin' you're saved."

"Yeah, but I'm new at it."

He smiled. "Do ya need a word from the Lord?"

After that moment in the bookstore, I sure needed something. "Yeah, maybe . . ."

The preacher took my hand, closed his eyes. He prayed for God to bless me and use me in a mighty way. He asked God to ease what was troubling my heart, so I guess my face had been telling on me.

On the train back, I recalled my last night in Telanoo when I prayed to see what I was fighting, to understand why we had to find the armor of God. A shiver of cold coursed through my veins. Then I remembered Dr. Dale saying that a warrior's shield can be shattered during the initial attack on the front lines. My faith sure felt fractured.

Once off the train, I stood at the station near a street lamp, watching how people hailed cabs so I'd know how to do it. I hailed one, jumped in, and gave the cabbie the address. I kept an eye on his expression in the rearview mirror and made small talk about the weather until I got back to Murlough House. I gave the mini version of the service and went to my room. The others knew better than to follow.

I wanted to tell someone about what happened at the bookstore, but couldn't bring myself to do it. They'd think I'd lost my mind—I wasn't so sure myself.

I clicked off the light and lay there in the dark, eyes wide and staring at nothing, afraid to sleep. Night devos went on down the hall, and I prayed that they'd keep singing until I fell asleep. But even the songs couldn't drown out the words meant for me and me alone: *You'll never find it.*

How'd that thing get into my world anyway? How'd he know where I was? Had Sahara's fire opened the veil to the dark side, and did he watch me build my fire for God on the Hill of Slane and follow me all the way to Dublin? Was he right about the sword?

I buried my face in my pillow. *God, why don't you tell me where it is?*

Chapter 14

WE couldn't find it. We drove back roads, got blocked in by cows, and pulled over in graveyards to search the lonely, isolated hills of central Ireland. Leap Castle could not be found.

Slightly offended, Dr. Eloise said, "These directions are vague. Obviously this isn't a popular tourist stop. Don't expect much of a gift shop."

We stopped at a pub and asked directions from an old farmer. He gave them, but his accent was so thick I couldn't understand him. The Stallards thanked him and pulled out.

Dr. Dale turned to his wife. "Did you get that?"

"Nary a word. But his finger pointed down that road."

We drove for a couple of miles.

"Have you children been working on your limericks?" she asked, trying to lighten the mood.

"I have mine," Reece flipped open her journal and read:

Me write a limerick? What do I say?
I'm happy to see my friend Mei!
The land is so green,
The greenest I've seen.
I like the museums—
I'm glad we got to see 'em.
The food is tops,
There are lots of coffee shops.

"I know this is too long, but I'm the mouth of the bunch!"

"Hey, that was it!" Rob said.

We turned around at the next farm road and backtracked to square stone gates whose iron doors stood open against a white sky. The van bumped down the rutted gravel drive. A solitary tower rose ahead. The castle came into full view, and Dr. Dale slammed on the brakes. For the second time in a week, we'd come upon a place that left us speechless. Nothing I can say in the way of description would explain what I felt. . . .

Leap Castle was an ivy-covered shell of smoky plaster and stone surrounded by lonely blue-gray hills. It was flat along the front and two stories high with a three-story tower in the middle. There was ugliness in its wide tower: a single church window over the door and a narrow window above that. Two pointed decorations at the front corners looked like horns, or ears. Some buildings have faces—a door for the mouth and window-eyes looking down at you. Leap Castle was blind. No eyes, the central church window a slack mouth, its stony ears perked and listening for something across silent hills.

A shell of a left wing threw the whole house off balance; its six windows were broken out. Stone fences angled out toward us in front of the wings. The chimneys were ready to topple. Mist crept along the front; dead trees stood inside the roofless left wing; moss crawled up the walls; ivy dripped from the tower. It was as if the earth was reclaiming it—digesting it day by day.

"Whoa . . . ," Skid whispered, "this is one sinister place."

"Gift shop closed for all eternity," Rob remarked.

"You got that right, Ballyrob," said Skid—dead serious.

"A spiritual vacuum," murmured Dr. Eloise.

"Kowai!" Mei said. "Scary!"

"This is our last place to look," I said gloomily. I couldn't imagine finding the sword of the Lord here.

"It looks like it was bombed," Reece said desperately.

"Destruction by fire actually, almost a century ago," Dr. Eloise commented. "Before we go in, we pray."

I heard the whisper in my head: *You'll never find it!*

"Good idea," Dr. Dale agreed.

As they prayed, I listened but kept an eye on the castle. In one way Leap Castle had nothing of what would usually scare a person: no glowing lights in the window, no swampy moat, no tall threatening towers. It was a blind nothing standing in silhouette against a white sky. Actually the place seemed to open its stony arms: *Come on in. Nothing here. Looking for something, eh? You'll never find it.*

Not a soul was around. The front door was locked, but a soggy gangplank had been propped against the front left window. One by one we sidestepped up the rain-slick boards. Mei and I kept hold of Reece until she made it to the threshold. Dr. Eloise spoke in a hushed tone as we looked around the weed-infested room with no ceiling.

"From what I gathered, this castle was a stronghold for the powerful, warlike clan, the MacMerrits—the last to surrender to the British in the 1600s."

My ears perked—*feet crunching on gravel.* I ran to the gangplank. Coming down the path was a medium-size man with long, gray hair. "We're closed!" he barked at me.

Dr. Dale rushed to the opening. "Good day, sir! We saw no one around. We're from the States. Touring castles." He pulled out a handful of bills. "A few minutes of your time?"

The man eyed the money. "I have to be leavin' soon."

Dr. Dale put the bills in the caretaker's hand. "I see from the two new windows over there that you're renovating. That must cost a few bob, eh? The children here are students on an educational tour. Ten minutes and a little history of the place?"

The man's frazzled expression mellowed. "The history, well . . ." He started in with dates and names and when the clan died out, which I pretty much glossed over as we followed him from the left wing to the main room. "Below the keep here is a network of dungeons cut from rock. A treasure is supposedly buried here by a lord who went mad and forgot where he hid it. Tales of torture and death fill our history."

"Have you seen the dungeons?" Rob asked.

"The passages are bricked up."

"So no one has seen inside since they were bricked up?" I asked eagerly.

"I reckon not, lad. It's all rot and decay under the keep."

"This is historical fact?" Dr. Dale asked.

"The passage is there." His face screwed up in a humorless grin. "The treasure *could* be a tale, mind you," he surveyed the walls, "but me grandfather was here his very self when they cleared out the *spiked* dungeon, there off the chamber of the Bloody Chapel." He pointed to an empty corner. "That's where they'd throw their enemies, one atop another and leave 'em to die slow and horrible in the bloody awful company of corpses. Fact. When the place was gutted in the twenties, they hauled out three whole carts of bones."

We moved to the corner and looked down the deep square hole. The owner eyed Reece and Mei slyly. "Leap Castle: where the MacMerrits brought their brides and their prisoners. I guess yer history lesson here is, ya shan't mess with the MacMerrits."

"But they all died out, didn't they?" Rob asked.

"There's a few left. Most've scattered to the winds."

Even Skid's face had gone slack looking into the spiked dungeon. "The Bloody Chapel?"

"Where one of the clan killed his brother at the altar in the middle of services."

"Killed his own brother?" Reece asked in horror.

"Ran a sword through him."

"Sword?" I asked. "What kind?"

"No idea, lad." The owner saw he had our attention. "But of all the tales of me ole castle, none is so unnerving, none so chillin' as the foul-smellin' demon that haunts the tower stair—an evil creature, one that embodies all the old horrors of the place."

"Are we speaking historically?" Dr. Dale asked critically.

He shrugged. "A lady of the manor dabbled in the black arts, and she swore to seein' it."

Reece asked, "Have *you* ever seen or heard anything?"

"Felt a deathly chill once right before me ladder tipped. Almost broke me neck."

As I remembered Dr. O'Leary's reference to bone-chilling cold, Skid shook his head skeptically. "Yeah, you hear that all the time—people feeling cold when evil spirits are around. What's up with that?"

"Dunno," the man said honestly. "I gave it thought after it come over me—put meself in a devil's head to figger him out—and here's what I come up with." He shifted his weight to one side. "If I was so unfortunate as to be one of the damned, yet so fortunate to escape the pit for a short while, I'd surely find a place with nothing of flames and screaming about it. If I couldn't find a body to occupy, then I'd welcome cold and silence and emptiness . . . if it were me escaping from the pit of Hell." He looked directly at me. "Wouldn't *you*, lad?"

Uncontrollable fear shot through me. I fought the trembling so the others wouldn't see. The unnatural chill and the walls washed in the pale light of the lone church window took me back to Old Pilgrim's basement.

The Stallards wouldn't let me pick through the place—the floors and some of the walls were unstable. The castle had been scavenged by treasure hunters and ghost seekers. I asked about the walled-up dungeons. Dr. Eloise answered with a question, "Honestly, Elijah, who would bury such a wonderful sword?"

"The guide at Ballymeade said it was done all the time," I argued. "A sword could be buried when its owner died."

She smiled mysteriously. "Well, the owner of our sword is very much alive."

Still, it killed me to get in the van and drive away. "If it's not there, where is it?" I cried. "Maybe it was the sword MacMerrit used to kill his brother. We should have asked the guy about *that* sword. Maybe those walled-up dungeons are where all the magics of the ages are buried!"

Dr. Dale simply said, "We will not find it here."

We drove southwest into the sun. Silence hung like fog in the van—we were all thinking the same thing. We'd exhausted our resources. I expected the Stallards to say something cheery or uplifting, but Dr. Dale kept his eyes on the sunset. After a while he looked at the map, "We need to find lodging soon."

We found a shamrock B&B and settled in for the night. Since it was our last night with Mei, the Stallards let us kids hang out in one room until late. Sahara would be meeting her at the airport the next day. After a card game or two, the conversation turned to God. Reece read some Scripture about how everyone needs God, and people who don't know him dream up other gods to fill the gaps in their hearts. She explained how Jesus died on the cross to pay for our sins and fill the gaps. I sat on the bed with my back against the wall and watched Reece do her thing—her face glowing with love as she talked about Jesus. Skid threw in stuff too. I wanted to have a say, but I was new at it, so I mostly listened with a lump in my throat, a hollow darkness in my gut, and an echo in my head: *you'll never find it.*

Mei was having a really hard time. "I know in my mind it is true. I understand about the God of the universe. I know the world was not an accident. I believe in *Souzousha.*" Her head dropped. "But my heart is torn in two. My parents, my family, and my friends in Japan—no one else wants me to believe."

Reece hugged Mei and explained what the Stallards had said about having a little shield. "A little faith is okay to start with. A little shield works just fine if we stand side by side."

"Hey," I said finally, "before we turn in, let's have a devo. How 'bout a verse from the *Warrior?*"

Rob said, "Dr. Dale said that the pages of the *Cathach* go from Psalm 30:10 to chapter 105:13."

"I'll read the last verse since this is our last night together." I smiled at Mei, "For a while, anyway."

Skid punched in the numbers and read to himself. "Hmm."

"What's it say?" Mei asked eagerly.

Skid handed the Quella to me. I read, "'They wandered from nation to nation, from one kingdom to another.'"

I looked at Skid. He nodded. "That's us, Creek. The new wave."

I was anxious to see Mom again, but I wasn't crazy about telling her our quest was a total bust. I kept myself pumped at the prospect of getting to know a potential new grandma. Rob and I hadn't really talked about it. I didn't want to get my hopes up. But as the next morning rolled around, I started imagining a new grandma. It'd be strange, but my life at this point was as loopy as a roundabout.

In the thick fog, we barely found the one-lane road to Seven Avon Place. Our van seemed to be drifting on a cloud toward nothing. Trading glances as we crossed the narrow spit of land, we silently worried that Dr. Eloise would miss the road and drop us all into the icy sea. Ghostly trees appeared ahead and soon covered us over. We drove down the lane in silence.

A square, gray shape appeared. There were no lights on.

"I'll get my mom." I ran up to the door and knocked. For a long minute no one answered. I peeked through the side windows. Empty. I didn't knock a second time; I tried the door. It was unlocked. I stepped in on cracked marble tiles covered with dust from fallen plaster and neglect. Tall rooms to the left and right stood empty. It was freezing cold.

"Mom?"

I swept down the hall in the same way I cover ground in Telanoo—eyes and ears on alert. The layout was similar to Murlough House, a wide hall running through to the back with rooms right and left. *The kitchen! If anyone's here, there'll be tea and cookies laying around, stuff in the fridge.*

The kitchen at the back of the house was bare—no stove, no refrigerator. *This hasn't been used in ages! Where's my mom?!*

I covered the first floor in a matter of seconds: dining room, a kind of ballroom, a huge laundry room, bathrooms. All bare. Panic rose as I shot up the stairs and covered the second floor. Creaking doors opened to empty rooms. *Ruthie and that man and that baby don't live here! No one lives here!!*

I sailed up the next flight of steps and ran into another large, empty room with bars on the windows. "Mom!!" I yelled. My voice echoed. *Knock, knock.* I waited.

Knock, knock, knock.

My mom's voice came through the wall. "Elijah?"

"Mom!" Horror swept through me. *She's trapped in another dimension!*

Her voice came loud and clear. "The other stairs, Elijah, the servant stairs! Go back down."

"Get a grip!" I yelled at myself. I ran back to the second floor and found another set of steps at the back of the house. A door squeaked open above me; I dashed up.

The woman who met me at the top hardly looked like my mom. Her face was drained of color, her hair was in a messy knot, and her eyes were swollen and sad. Weakly she said, "Hi, hon."

"Mom?!"

She came to me and dropped her head on my shoulder.

"Did you find her?" I whispered.

She whispered back, "We'll talk later."

Mom let me into a warm little apartment with nice homey decorations. Breakfast dishes still sat on the table. Ruthie was rocking her baby.

Mom thanked Ruthie and hugged her a long time.

I picked up Mom's luggage by the door and headed down the steps. "Let's go."

Saying good-bye to Mei was tough. While we'd been working on our school projects, she'd made each of our first initials on squares of real parchment with fancy designs like in the *Book of Kells.*

After a bucket full of apologies for being weak on English, Mei gave us her limerick:

> *Ireland I have never seen.*
> *I like travel with* Amerika-jin.
> *A very long* ryokou
> *To haunted Leap-*jou
> *Is scary at Halloween!*

We gave her a round of applause.

"I may never see you again," she cried to all of us.

"Yes, you will!" Reece cried back.

Mei handed out her gifts. "Don't forget me! Please come to Japan. I need your help to tell my friends about God."

"We will, I promise!" Reece said. "We'll come!"

The Stallards swapped looks.

Sahara showed up, and we all gave Mei one last hug. I hugged her extra hard and whispered, "Have faith in *Souzousha.*"

We reluctantly handed Mei over to Sahara, went through security, and were airborne in an hour.

Skid was so impressed with his fancy letter *M* that he announced, "People, I may have to upgrade my name like Rob did. Yeah, I think I will. I'm too old for nicknames."

Our plane shot up through the green mists of Ireland, and in a minute a whole country disappeared.

When we leveled off at thirty thousand feet, I said, "Um, Mom . . ."

"I know. You want to know if you have a new grandmother. My . . . mother is alive but in very bad health."

"Did you meet her?"

Her head wobbled tiredly. "I saw her, but she didn't see me. She wouldn't have known me. When we get home, I'll explain everything to the whole family. I have to get my thoughts together, okay?"

"Sure, Mom." I wanted to ask more—like if we were coming back to see Grandma—but she was too broken up.

The mood was quiet. Reece wrote in her journal. I fiddled

with the beautiful *E* Mei had made me. Dr. Dale started eating solid food again. I fell asleep, and the next thing I knew, we were over green valleys and long, rust-colored mountains: the Appalachians. In a couple hours, we'd be home. It was over.

I saw Skid writing and asked, "Hey, is that your limerick, Marcus?"

"It stinks."

"Let's have it. Mom'll want to read them all."

He'd written one thing each of us might say about the trip:

> *Rob: Ireland was one big, foggy day.*
> *Mei: In Ireland you taught me to pray.*
> *Me: I changed my name.*
> *Reece: Elijah lit the flame.*
> *Elijah: And the sword is still hidden away.*

Chapter 15

CAMP Mudjokivi looked strangely unfamiliar. Sand had been hauled into the future volleyball court. The leaves were mostly gone, the pool was covered, and a light snow had fallen. The twins had cut their hair with their new scissors while Mom was gone. Dad was ready to grovel for forgiveness for letting it happen, but she hardly even noticed.

After dinner Mom sat the twins and me down in the living room to tell her story. "About thirty-five years ago, a young Irish girl named Isabel had some very strict parents. She grew up to be a very pretty girl, and they thought she might get into trouble and embarrass the family. So they sent her away to live on an island, a place run by the church where they took girls with problems. She was so unhappy there that she tried to escape many times. Finally she succeeded. She ran off with a young man and got married. But he wasn't her religion, so when her parents found her, they took her back to the island. She had twins, a boy and a girl, who were taken and put up for adoption."

"You and Uncle Dorian," I said.

"That's right, and now she is very sick from all she suffered at that place. Sometimes old people have trouble remembering things. Well, your Grandma Isabel can't remember much anymore. I went to the old people's home where she lives and looked in on her. See girls, I know who she is, but she wouldn't know me." Mom made a strange smile and shrugged. "Who am I to her? A stranger, that's all."

"Did you take a picture, so we could see her?" Nori asked.

"She didn't look so well, hon. I can tell you she was slender and had some gray in her hair and a small face like me." Mom got a distant look. "I don't know what color her eyes were. I didn't get that close. But I did get to meet a wonderful young woman who helps people find their parents. Her name is Ruthie. Guess what? She took me shopping one day, and I brought you back a souvenir." From behind the couch cushion, she brought two woolly toy lambs with silver shamrock necklaces fastened on. She put the necklaces on the girls. "Don't they look pretty! Well, you can know that you had a beautiful grandmother who would have loved you very much—" her voice broke, "if she had known you."

When the twins ran off to look at their necklaces in the mirror, Mom turned to me. "Elijah, your father and I want to talk with you about something."

Uh-oh . . .

When the girls were all the way upstairs, she turned to me and took my hands in hers. "I know you are interested in church things now, but . . ." She started shaking her head.

"What?"

"I can't tell you everything that happened to my mother, but this I know. We, her children, were stolen from her—by her church. She was kept a virtual prisoner in that awful place to work like a slave and make money—for her church. Separated from her husband, isolated from the outside world—"

Strange. Sounds a lot like Kate Dowland's story, I thought.

"She lost her mind and was sent to an asylum. That's where I went, to see her. All this was done by her church."

I see where this conversation's going. "Mom, mine's diff—"

She squeezed my hands roughly. "Listen! You'll soon be an adult, Elijah. You should be making your own choices. But I—your father and I—strongly recommend that you not get involved with any kind of established religion. You're a good boy. You don't need a religion to teach you right from wrong. We've done that." Her voice sounded desperate. "You have a belief system that you developed on your own. As long as you are sincere in what you believe, Elijah, that's all that matters. You're a good son. Any problems you have in life, you can always come to us. Family's important. Anything that divides a family—whether it's a church or—well, it can never be a good thing, can it, to tear a family apart?"

"No," I said.

She patted my knee. "Good."

Chapter 15

On the outside my life hurtled back to normal.
The Stallards sent a packet of castle pictures, museum
pamphlets, a copy of the *Ogham* alphabet, and a letter. Dr.
Dale wrote:

Dear World Travelers!

*First order of business: with regard to your research paper,
Elijah, I believe your Latin instructor may have set you up. There
is no consistently held opinion on the extent to which Rome may or
may not have subjugated Ireland. And consider this technicality:
Ireland was called Hibernia at the time Caesar ruled. So in the
literal sense, he most certainly did not invade Ireland. We relish
scholarship but do not envy you this assignment. Good luck!*

*One interesting tack you might take, related to the pamphlet
we showed you: one Roman soldier of note did conquer Ireland—
Patrick. Remember? He was the son of a Roman official and a
soldier of the cross. He conquered Ireland, not with the clash of
metal, but with the sword of the Spirit.*

*Regarding the sword—if Patrick's fire is all we see of the Lord's
flaming sword, perhaps it is enough. The fire burned brightly in
Ireland: at Murlough House, on a street corner in Dublin, and one
glorious night on the Hill of Slane.* (I pictured Dr. Dale smiling
as he wrote, slugging coffee from his gasoline-smelling
flask.) *We are discouraged but not defeated. Spending time with you
wonderful people was worth every minute.*

*Thanks to you, Elijah, we deciphered the slashes on the
shield. They are* Ogham *script, as you thought. The word is*
creidim, *Gaelic for "faith." You are a very discerning young man!*

Interestingly this alphabet was used only in the British Isles and only for a few centuries, the time of Patrick and the peregrini, *including Columba, the one who fought—perhaps with our shield of faith—to have the Scriptures in his own hands. Isn't it curious, children, that in ages past men fought to the death to have even one painstaking portion of the Word? Today Bibles collect dust. Perhaps they understood what our generations don't. Yes, perhaps as a species we are devolving.*

If we can assist you in recovering the helmet, let us know.

All our best,

The Stallards

PS. The snafu with Mr. Cravens compels us to give an extra word of caution. If a stranger should come to Magdeline asking questions about armor, notify us immediately!

PPS. What about the arm? Was there not a right arm found at some point?

Emma Stone was still a problem. She asked me a million questions about Ireland and ignored whatever Reece had to say. I hated to think it, but it seemed like she'd been helping Reece all along just as a way to get to me. Bummer.

There were two bright spots my first week back though: first, I won the cross-country meet by a mile. Coach still couldn't believe that I hadn't trained before and said I was a shoo-in for regionals. Maybe state too. Coach and I were on solid ground again. Bright spot number two was— ironically—Latin. I got a B on my paper (which *proves* there is a God), but that wasn't the best part. As I said before, Rob's class always went to lunch right before the bell rang. He'd do his hula dance and mouth words like weeky weeny weedy wooky. I never got tired of it, and he never let me down. But by November Abner had caught on that I watched the door and cracked up the same minute every day. One day she kept squinting at the clock around that time. I thought that she was sick of us, or just hankering for her daily peanut butter and crackers. At exactly twenty till, she stopped writing on the board and went to the corner by the door. I knew what was about to happen. Rob sauntered down the hall between Miranda Varner, who was Marcus's love interest, and the infamous Justin Brill. I was ready to frantically wave Rob a warning when I thought of the rubber ducky. *Now's my chance! Here it comes, Wingate. Payback!*

I grinned like a baboon just to egg him on. He was wooky-weekying as big as you please when Abner jutted her stiff neck from behind the door and caught him in the act.

"Disturb my class, will you?" Miss Abner raged.

A weeky-weeky smile froze on Rob's face. Justin log-jammed behind him and grunted. Miranda sped ahead as Miss Abner shouted, "Tooooo the OFFICE, Missster BRILL!"

Justin's brows knotted and his mouth went into an oval of disbelief. Rob's hula hands dropped to his sides, and he stepped away from Justin like he had cooties. Blind-as-a-bat Abner marched into the hall and stuck her finger in Justin's face. "How dare you disturb my class! Don't think you've fooled me!"

Rob turned on one heel like a soldier, his jaw clamped shut against an explosion of giggles. I shoved all my papers off my desk as an excuse to duck under my desk and guffaw.

Every day after that, Rob would pass by as stiff as a private in boot camp, Brill would scowl in my direction, and I'd laugh to myself. And since Rob came out smelling like a rose, he still had one coming from me. Maybe I'd wait for his baptism and drop in an angry snapping turtle right before the amen.

November waned; I couldn't sleep for thinking about the sword. I had to get back to the junkyard to see if there were any metal remains in Dowland's charred car. That next Saturday I headed out on my bike, wearing a heavy jacket to keep out the cold drizzle. By the time I got to the junkyard, my hair was dripping, and my ears and fingers were numb. The gate was locked, but the fence drooped from where the men had leaped over to put out the fire.

Dowland's car was a blackened shell. The seats were piles of ash. The trunk yawned open to show more black ash in no particular shape. By the time I'd checked the inside, my jacket and jeans were smeared with soot. Mom would wonder what I'd been up to. I didn't want to worry her. She was spending a lot of time on the couch, staring out the window. She fixed mostly frozen dinners and didn't eat much. The girls didn't know what was wrong. Dad explained: "Mom is going to be sad for a while, girls. Her trip to Ireland was very hard. Be good helpers so she can feel better fast."

Dismal darkness fell around me in the junkyard. I had to get back or Mom would worry—if she even noticed I was gone. I stopped by Dowland's on the way back, but it had been sold, emptied, and locked. Dowland's legacy was a dead end. *You'll never find it.* The voice had never left, and I wrestled over talking to someone about it. But who? I couldn't tell Reece, not until I understood it better myself. Mom and Dad? Not a chance. There wasn't doubt one in my mind—I could never explain to them what happened. The Stallards were in Chicago. I didn't know Reece's minister all that well. Who could help me fight off the dark side?

Dom.

Once I'd worked up the courage to spill my guts to macho-military Dom Skidmore and take whatever he dished out, I bundled up and walked along Magdeline's dark, abandoned main street toward the Skidmores' condo. I wondered, *Since there really is another world, a spirit world, and since the creatures behind the veil can pass through to us, then it would seem pretty important to be protected from them. Are they watching me through the veil as I walk alone tonight? What kind of powers do they have? Do they know my thoughts?* I began to see the point of having the armor of God.

It's real, I said over and over to get it through my thick skull. God, Satan, Heaven, and Hell. It's not just religion. It's real. My knees got kind of weak. If that's true, then why is there only one guy in my whole town who can help me?

The whole idea knocked the wind out of me. For crying out loud, there're all kinds of people to protect us against crime and general meanness: Officer Taylor and other cops, the armed forces with their weapons and planes and bombs, detectives, CIA, FBI. We have parking meter cops and even dog cops!

Forget the criminal hordes! What about the evil hordes beyond the veil? Who fights them—one person in all of Magdeline?!

A car pulled into the Skidmore driveway. I approached it. Dom was getting out when he saw me. "What are you doing out so late?"

"I need to talk to you—privately."

He studied me. "The car's still warm."

"That'd be good."

I'd practiced how I would explain about Liam, about the voice and the eyes of hate, how he might have been talking about the book. But I knew in my heart he wasn't—that the words weren't really coming from him.

Dom heard me out and nodded thoughtfully. "Old Serpent got you alone and scared the crap out of you, didn't he? He had you in his crosshairs and took his shot."

I admitted sheepishly, "I did ask God to let me see."

"See what?"

"What's out there . . . you know, the enemy."

"Better watch what you ask God for. You just might get it." His look went serious and dark. He paused. "Why do you think it happened?"

"So I'd know it's real?"

"You didn't know evil was real? Didn't know Hell and damnation was real?"

"I wasn't sure. My parents don't talk about that stuff."

"Well, now you know. No turning back."

"Yeah," I murmured halfheartedly.

We sat there looking at the garage door lit up by headlights. He asked, "Do you wish you could go back and pretend that life was all about sports and cute girls?"

"Sort of," I admitted.

"No you don't. You're a deep kid, Elijah. You're made of strong stuff. Hold your position."

I told him I'd had a dream here and inkling there and still wasn't sure what it all meant.

"Guess you need a Quella."

I nodded. "I'll start saving up."

"Better yet—" he popped one out of his glove box and tossed it to me. "Your mission has just taken a hit. Start gathering intelligence."

"Wow. You mean it?"

"Hold your position now."

"Yessir."

Chapter 16

MOM'S disposition was changing. She griped about my phone calls to the Stallards. She got moody when I went to church with Reece—even though she said it was my choice—and harped on me about neglecting my homework. But going to cross-country meets was just fine with her.

It was after she walked in on one of our rare powwows at the lodge that she lowered the boom. She called me and Dad into the living room again. "Elijah, I guess I didn't make myself clear before. Your trip to Ireland was a great adventure, but the search for those old armor pieces—is over. You didn't find what you were looking for. That's all right. But now we want you to concentrate on your future: your studies and extracurricular activities."

What?! I looked at Dad. He didn't exactly agree—I could see that—but he wanted to keep the peace. He wanted the old Jodi Creek back. *She'll change her mind,* I thought hopefully. *She'll get over it.* It seemed like I was standing on the Cliffs of Morte again. Mom's words were like a North Atlantic blast.

She went on, "And more responsibilities at camp." She smiled. "Someday Camp Mudj will be yours! Don't think that we're not grateful to the Stallards for all the time they've spent with you. But they're just a couple of strangers interested in relics. They're not spending all this money on you kids for nothing; they want something in return."

Now you're sounding like Uncle Dorian, I thought angrily.

"So are we clear?" she asked.

"Ditch everything, that's what you're saying!" I snapped.

"Not everything! Goodness, no. You have family and friends, camp, school, and cross-country. Your future!!"

Only days before, Dom had asked me if I ever wanted to go back and pretend that life was nothing more than sports and cute girls. Now my weak-willed answer disgusted me.

The next couple of days, I felt like I was walking through an Irish fog. I gathered the others at my locker, grabbing Reece before Emma could glom onto her for the day. I told them what Mom had said.

"That's not the whole story," Rob informed me. "What she told Dad was a lot more gruesome. Did she tell you that Seven Avon Place had been called the Isle of Magdeline? And did she tell you that when the house was closed a decade ago, a hundred unmarked graves were discovered?"

No place is safe, came a voice in my head. *No one can be trusted—no one.*

I felt like a traitor dialing the Stallards' number from Reece's apartment so my parents wouldn't know.

Dr. Dale answered. I cut to the chase. "I have to know. What are you getting out of this?"

Long pause. "The truth."

"It has to be more than that."

"Does it?"

"My mom says so."

"It didn't go well for your mother in Ireland. We've done a bit of research on Seven Avon Place."

"Formerly the Isle of Magdeline," I said, agitated. "Mom said it was all the church's fault. She said I shouldn't have anything to do with church and that I'm good enough already."

Long pause. "I should have warned you. But," he cleared his throat, "I didn't know it would happen this soon."

"What would happen?"

"The testing of your faith. The tribulations."

"Reece's minister told me that God gives tests," I said. "Is that what you mean?"

"Yes—not finding the sword, your mother's objections. Good and evil are constantly at odds for your soul. God wants to save you; Satan wants to destroy you."

"How do you know who's doing what, and when?"

"Sometimes you don't. Not until later."

"Oh, great. Well, Mom said that anything that breaks up families can't be good. So the church can't be good."

"God created families, Elijah. It is not his will that they be divided." He took a long, tired breath. "Perhaps Eloise and I should have spent more time on the pitfalls of the armor quest. But this . . . this is unique."

"Um," I hesitated, "there was another test."

"What do you mean?"

"You may not believe me . . ."

"I will."

"I think the devil talked to me."

I thought he'd freak when I said that, but he just said anxiously, "Dear Heaven. I'm just considering the nature of your quest—arming a generation. What did the entity say?"

I retold the story, explaining how the voice from Liam said, "You'll never find it."

There was a long pause.

"Dr. Dale?"

"I'm still here. What did you say to . . . it?"

"I left."

"Good. Never address the evil ones without the authority of Jesus' name, and never ever *directly* rebuke them, Elijah. Instructions about this are in the book of Jude and elsewhere in the Bible. You do have a Bible, don't you?"

"I have a Quella."

"Good, that will help you find the words you need quickly. When Donovan's in the States again, I'll have him contact you. He has expertise in this area beyond my own."

I wasn't sure how to break it to him except straight. "The reason I called is that my mom doesn't want me involved in the church or in the armor search anymore. It's because of how the church ruined my grandma's life."

"Elijah, there's the church and then there's *the church*. There are people who go into buildings with religious names on them every Sunday. Most people see that as the church."

"But I know it's not a building full of people." Reece had talked about this before.

"Oh, that it were that simple. The church, Elijah, is invisible. It is made up of those who love God with heart, soul, mind, and strength."

Did I belong in that category? I was way curious about God and his armor and what he wanted me to do in the world—not to mention being curious about the devil. But all this heart and soul stuff—that was asking a lot.

"It's a process, learning to love God," Dr. Dale cut in on my thoughts. "Don't judge yourself. You've started the journey, Elijah; that's what matters."

"So what about Halloween when the walls between the worlds grow thin? What's that mean?"

"You're quoting the pagans. The whole truth is that the veil between the worlds is *always* thin. When you call to God, he is there. By the same token, if you open a door to the abyss by letting evil into your life, you'll discover that it is eager to claim you. Good and evil do not rest; and like the winds on the Cliffs of Morte, evil does not forewarn you. So don't forget, the veil between the worlds is *always* thin."

"My mom says I have to give up looking for the armor. What do I do about that?" There was a long pause again. I felt guilty hitting him with so much bad news.

"Take some time, Elijah."

"And why did you stop eating on the trip? I'm sorry, but I need to know what's going on."

"I was fasting and praying," he answered.

"Why?"

His voice came through the phone stern and severe, "Because of Rob's disbelief, Sahara's pagan influence over Mei, Reece's health, Marcus's ego, and your lack of understanding of the simplest truths of the faith. You five are completely unprepared for the task ahead. Not one of you has the vaguest idea what kind of spiritual and physical danger you are in."

And here I'd become a Christian so things would be better.

Chapter 17

░░

I went deep into Telanoo to a little canyon—smaller and more isolated than those in Council Cliffs. Rocks hung over, dripping with icicles like daggers, like crystal swords aimed down at me from Heaven. Some were taller than me. Here and there when the wind blew, a little icicle would break off and shatter the quiet. At the end of the ravine was a frozen waterfall, a wide line of icy trickles.

I leaned against the cliff, tucked safely behind the crystal swords. They seemed like a dirty trick: God showed me a thousand swords, but I couldn't have the one I wanted—his sword. It was time for a confrontation.

The wind was like ice; my fingers and toes ached. Darkness descended, and I waited for the Presence. I waited, but he never came. Everything I believed and felt was crumbling, breaking off, and crashing to the ground. *Maybe the world would have been better off without Patrick burning his fire of faith, without that Dublin preacher and his motley crew embarrassing themselves on the streets. Maybe the Stallards would be better off peddling Babylonian demon heads on the antiquities market instead of looking for armor pieces lost in a backwater town like Magdeline.* The more I thought, the angrier I got.

My grandma would have had a better chance on the mean streets than in a church-run slave camp. Mom would have been better off never knowing. Maybe Reece would be better off giving up on trying to be so cheery all the time. Face the truth. Her life will never be all that great.

Suddenly I was standing beneath the ice swords with my head thrown back. "Just who do you think you are? I'm not afraid of you and what you can do to me! You ruined my grandma! You hurt my mom! You crippled Reece for life! And Mei's in the clutches of a family of witches who, by the way, seemed really nice! You could have fixed it. I've seen you work! You could still fix everything if you wanted to. Well, I'm not holding my breath, Master of Breath!"

Silence.

I trembled, rage boiling up in me. "This is not what I wanted! You think you're going to mess up my life like the others? You think you can scare me with demons! You have another think coming!"

Silence.

The air seemed to thin out; it was so cold and brittle that I could hardly breathe. *There's plenty of air,* I told myself nervously, *it's just cold and it hurts my lungs.* My chest tightened, my heart ached. I fought off panic. *Is he going to kill me for smarting off?* "Are you?" I gasped out loud. "Are you going to kill me like Dr. Eloise said you could?" The wind suddenly rose. I ducked under the cliff to get out of the wind and wondered if an earthquake was next. Would the cliffs collapse and trap me, crush me, and send me off into eternity? He could do it if he wanted to. *No one can stop you!* I stumbled back, pressing my hand against the cold stone, bracing for what was to come. I expected to feel smooth rock, but my fingers found grooves. *What is that?* Clicking on my flashlight, I examined the stone. *Claw marks? A bear waking up from hibernation, starving and grouchy, taking a swat at the world? Yeah . . . no.* These slashes were deep, chiseled with a tool. Clumped and irregular but definitely man-made.

Suddenly my mind changed course. *Could it be . . . Indian!?* The Moravian Delawares, the two boys who'd lived out their lives in Hermits' Cave. *What if they'd been here? What if this was a message from them? How cool would that be?* I forgot about my argument with God and studied the marks a long time. *I need to show these to the Stallards.* There were too many to memorize. *I'll come back,* I told the message in stone.

Heading back toward home, I kept the flashlight on the ground. *Well, God, if you won't talk to me, maybe the Indians will.* The frozen stream like a curving, silver arrow guided my way. In an hour I came up behind what would be a new sand volleyball court. *Dad'll have to put up a privacy fence,* I thought practically, back to my old self. *Who wants to go out of bounds in volleyball and fall headlong into a cemetery and get RIP permanently stamped on his forehead?*

By the time I hit the porch, I was too frozen to be mad at God and too excited about the Indian message to sleep. I showered until the bathroom was thick with fog, put on sweats, went downstairs, and kissed mom on the cheek like nothing had happened.

"It's cold out," I said.

"You feel warm."

"I used up all the hot water."

"You going to bed already? It's early."

"I'm beat."

"Are you feeling okay, hon?"

I hugged her. "Don't worry, Mom. I'm okay."

Upstairs, I threw the covers back and jumped in bed. Once the light was off, I was wide awake. A message from the hermits! A secret across time for me, Elijah Creek!

I was dressed and halfway to the shallow cave before dawn. This place was going to be mine alone. I'd think up a new name and not even Rob or Marcus would know about it. I'd taken a big piece of paper and one of the twins' big stubby pencils to make a rubbing. I'd noticed one of an Egyptian tomb in the Chicago museum vault and knew how it worked. I placed the paper over the stone and rubbed with the side of the pencil. The grooves appeared on the paper as white slashes on a gray surface. For good measure I made a sketch. I had the message in positive and negative form. By lunchtime these would be on their way to the Stallards. I called them from home when Mom was busy.

"It's Elijah," I said quietly. "I found some marks on a rock in Telanoo and I think it could be an Indian message."

"Is that so?"

"From the Moravian Delawares maybe."

"What makes you think that?"

"It's not far from Hermits' Cave, and the marks were made by people, but they're not letters." I was ready to hang up when something occurred to me. "You know what, the slashes kind of look like the sun rays on the shield of faith, only they're all bunched up. I'll send you the rubbing. But don't call me. I'll call you when the coast is clear."

My clan was in limbo. Emma was still glomming onto Reece to get to me. Marcus would meet me in the hall with a what's-up expression, and I'd have to shrug. He was hanging with Miranda more. One night in December, I called Dr. Eloise for an update on the rubbing.

"AB-so-LUTE-ly fascinating!" she squealed. "It's rather a puzzle, since not all of the vowels are present and we're dealing with old Gaelic carved roughly into a rock. But we put together the best combination we could. Incredible! And how this message got from Ireland to the Midwest fifteen hundred years ago is . . . well, unbelievable! It seems to say: The right hand of God is a shield—a prayer."

"You're kidding."

"Serious as a heart attack," she chirped. "Remember the story of Brendan the Navigator, how he set out in a boat with his fellow *peregrini,* asking God to guide him where he should go?"

"You're not saying they got this far?! *To Telanoo!?*"

"History hints that the *peregrini* may have made it to America, but no supporting evidence has existed that they reached so far inland—until now. For fear of sounding redundant, Elijah, please be very careful with whom you discuss this. And keep the site a secret for now."

After school and cross-country, I ran back to my hidden gorge, pumped up about the new mystery and determined to tell no one—not even Reece (because of Emma). What should I call my secret place? I took the Quella from my jacket to find where the Elijah in the Bible lived: Gilead.

I made a fire in Gilead. I'd forgiven God and wanted to talk again. *El-Telan-Yah, you're going to have to tell me what to do next. And while you're at it, could you explain that seven-thousand-mile wild goose chase? Okay . . . you don't have to. I'm not meaning to be bossy. But I'm your kid, aren't I? And parents get a kick out of telling their kids what to do and lecturing them. Keep in mind that I'm new at this, so be easy on me, okay?*

For a half hour I paced around Gilead to keep warm. *I'm listening.* I pulled out the Quella and read again about the shield of faith, thinking I'd missed something. *What exactly does* faith *mean?* I punched in the question and read: "Faith is being sure of what we hope for and certain of what we do not see." *Okay. The sword is somewhere but I can't see it. Invisible. Like the rock that kept me from falling off the Cliffs of Morte? I didn't see it, but I sure believe in it!*

After a while I began to see. Not the helmet and

sword—not yet—but a ton of other great things in my life. The lessons I'd learned at Farr Island, a cool trip to Ireland—purpose still unknown, God working a plan so Reece and Mei could be together again. And other things, invisible things I could see only because of my faith: Jesus dying on the cross for me, my sins forgiven, eternal life. And the dark side. I looked up to the narrow strip of sky above the rim of my gorge. *Hey, speaking of the dark side, one peek through the veil was enough.*

I paced the gorge. *So the sword is invisible? Do I have to see it with eyes of faith? Or is it visible but hidden in a secret place? As darkness fell a quiet wave of confidence swept through me, and I was certain—without knowing how—that I'd put my hand on the thing I hoped for. One day I'd see what I could not see.*

Two words echoed in my head: *secret place . . . secret place.* Excitedly I checked the Quella. The first two references meant nothing to me, but the third pierced right into my soul. I took off for home through the cold, bare woods of Telanoo, reciting his words over and over, my heart pumping: "'I will give you the treasures of darkness, riches stored in secret places, so that you may know that I am the LORD, the God of Israel, who summons you by name.'"

Elijah Creek & The Armor of God #6

THE ANGEL OF FIRE

ELIJAH'S enemies—seen and unseen—are at every turn.
One haunts him from the grave
One demands he give up the quest *and* his faith.
One has an eye on Reece.
One wants his treasure.
One wants him dead.

Still haunted by a demon's voice and with nothing but a vague promise from Scripture, Elijah becomes discouraged. Apparently there is no sword—maybe there never was. The helmet is lost, and all of their leads are exhausted.

Elijah becomes a fugitive from his own life. Hostile and reclusive, he discovers where the next clue is, but it may be too late. He's trapped. His family and friends don't know where he is. But two from beyond this world have their eye on Elijah and are vying for his soul. Who will he listen to? Will the secret and the quest die with him?

The search for the armor of God reaches a critical turning point; Elijah and his friends finally discover the shocking truth about the Stallards. And the whole armor, which has moved across continents and through time to an unbelievable hiding place, is waiting to be activated in the hearts of five teens from Magdeline, Ohio.

Ancient Truth

※※

(Page 11) "He will save his people from their sins."

Matthew 1:21

(Page 12) "Whoever wants to save his life will lose it, but whoever loses his life for me will find it."

Matthew 16:25

(Page 12) "What good is it, my brothers, if a man claims to have faith but has no deeds? Can such faith save him?"

James 2:14

(Page 12) "For it is by grace you have been saved, through faith."

Ephesians 2:8

(Page 12) "If you confess with your mouth, 'Jesus is Lord,' and believe in your heart that God raised him from the dead, you will be saved."

Romans 10:9

(Page 39) "Then the LORD said to me, 'You have made your way around this hill country long enough; now turn north.'"

Deuteronomy 2:3

(Page 48) "Take up the shield of faith, with which you can extinguish all the flaming arrows of the evil one."

Ephesians 6:16

(Page 49) "You, who through faith are shielded by God's power until the coming of the salvation that is ready to be revealed in the last time. In this you greatly rejoice, though now for a little while you may have had to suffer grief in all kinds of trials. These have come so that your faith—of greater worth than gold, which perishes even though refined by fire—may be proved genuine."

1 Peter 1:4-7

(Page 52) "At that time many will turn away from the faith and will betray and hate each other, and many false prophets will appear and deceive many people. Because of the increase of wickedness, the love of most will grow cold."

Matthew 24:10-12

(Page 53) "When the Son of Man comes, will he find faith on the earth?"

Luke 18:8

(Page 59) "I am your shield, your very great reward."

Genesis 15:1

(Page 64) "You are a shield around me."

Psalm 3:3

(Page 64) "My shield is God Most High."

Psalm 7:10

(Page 64) "We wait in hope for the LORD; he is our help and our shield."

Psalm 33:20

(Page 80) "These are the words of him who has the sharp, double-edged sword. I know where you live—where Satan has his throne. . . . Repent therefore! Otherwise, I will soon come to you and will fight against them with the sword of my mouth."

Revelation 2:12, 13, 16

(Page 121) "When you look up to the sky and see the sun, the moon and the stars—all the heavenly array—do not be enticed into bowing down to them and worshiping things the LORD your God has apportioned to all the nations under heaven."

Deuteronomy 4:19

(Page 130) "Why do the nations conspire and the peoples plot in vain? The kings of the earth take their stand and the rulers gather together against the LORD and against his Anointed One. . . . The One enthroned in heaven laughs; the Lord scoffs at them. . . . O LORD, how many are my foes! How many rise up against me! Many are saying of me, 'God will not deliver him.' But you are a shield around me, O LORD; you bestow glory on me and lift up my head. To the LORD I cry aloud, and he answers me from his holy hill!"

Psalms 2:1-4; 3:1-4

(Page 183) "Faith is being sure of what we hope for and certain of what we do not see."

Hebrews 11:1

(Page 184) "I will give you the treasures of darkness, riches stored in secret places, so that you may know that I am the LORD, the God of Israel, who summons you by name."

Isaiah 45:3

Creek Code

※※

Delaware
Langundowagan—(lahn-goon-do-wah-gahn) Peace

Irish Gaelic
Cathach—(kah-thukh) Warrior
Samhain—(sow-en) Irish holiday comparable to Halloween
Lough—(lockh) Lake
Ogham—(oh-yam) Ancient system of writing to keep records
Creidim—(kred-im) Faith

Greek
Machaira—(makh-ahee-rah) Short sword, dagger, or saber
Rhomphaia—(hrom-fah-yah) Large brandishing sword

Japanese
Gi—(ghee) A kanji character meaning righteousness
Obon—(oh-bone) Japanese festival of the dead
Souzousha—(soh-zoh-shah) Creator
Kowai—(ko-wah-ee) Scary
Daijoubu—(die-jo-boo) It's all right
Amerika-jin—(ah-meh-ree-ka-jeen) American(s)
Ryokou—(ryo-koh) A trip
-Jou—(joh) Castle

Latin
Peregrini—(peh-reh-gree-nee) Pilgrim
Veni, Vidi, Vici—(weeny weedy weeky) I came, I saw, I conquered

Author's Note

THERE is a five-thousand-year-old passage tomb at Newgrange in the shape of a cross.

The story of Patrick's fire on the Hill of Slane in defiance of the high kings of Tara probably did occur around 433 AD.

A book called the *Cathach* (meaning "warrior") is the oldest Irish manuscript known to exist. A few of its pages are lost. There is a lovely little bookstore named after it.

Sketchy evidence exists that the *peregrini,* particularly Brendan, may have made it across the Atlantic. I was almost finished with the book and had decided to use *Ogham* script for the shield when I read about etchings found in West Virginia that resemble the ancient script, used from around 300–700 AD. One possible translation of the mysterious message in stone is: The right hand of God is a shield—a prayer.

Ballymeade Castle is a fictionalized version of Bunratty Castle.

Dunluce Castle and Leap Castle both exist as described, though I fiddled with their history a bit. Leap Castle's awful story is supposedly true. Inside is the Bloody Chapel and a spiked dungeon where carts of bones were found.

And the veil between the worlds is thin—and not just at Halloween. Be aware of the darkness. Walk in the light.

Check out this other new series . . .

GAME ON!

Stephen D. Smith with Lise Caldwell

GAME ON! is a
sports fiction series
featuring young athletes
who must overcome
obstacles—on and off
the field. The characters
in these stories are
neither the best athletes
nor the underdogs.
These are ordinary kids
of today's culture—
characters you'll
identify with and
be inspired by.

RED CARD

0-7847-1438-X

RIVALS ON THE WAVES

STEPHEN D. SMITH

0-7847-1470-3

HIGH HURDLES

STEPHEN D. SMITH WITH LISE CALDWELL

0-7847-1439-8

FOURTH AND LONG

STEPHEN D. SMITH WITH LISE CALDWELL

0-7847-1471-1